Moby Dick IN 101 PAGES

By: Herman Melville

This Fresh and Concise Interpretation

By: Levi F. Barber

ContemplateBooks.com

"Connecting Modern Readers with the Classics"

Table of Contents

Chapter 1. Loomings[1]

Call me Ishmael.[2] Some years ago—never mind how long precisely—having little or no money in my wallet, and nothing particular to interest me on shore, I thought I would sail about a little and see the watery part of the world. Whenever it is a damp, drizzly November in my soul, I account it high time to get to sea as soon as I can. This is my substitute for pistol and ball[3]. Nothing is surprising in this. Almost all men would have very nearly the same feelings about the ocean as I do if they only knew it.

Now, when I say that I am in the habit of going to sea whenever I begin to grow hazy about the eyes, I do not mean to have it inferred that I ever go to sea as a passenger. For to go as a passenger, you must have a wallet, and a wallet is but a rag unless you have something in it. Besides, passengers get sea-sick—grow quarrelsome—don't sleep at nights—do not enjoy themselves much;—no, I never go as a passenger; nor, do I ever go to sea as a Commodore, or a Captain, or a Cook. I abandon the glory and distinction of such offices to those who like them. For my part, I reject all honorable, respectable toils, trials, and tribulations of every kind whatsoever. It is quite as much as I can do to take care of myself without taking care of ships. And as for going as a cook, though I confess there is considerable glory in that, a cook being a sort of officer on ship-board, yet somehow, I never fancied broiling fowls.

No, when I go to sea, I go as a simple sailor. True, they rather order me about some and make me jump from spar to spar[4], like a grasshopper in a May meadow. And at first, this sort of thing is unpleasant enough. It touches one's sense of honour, particularly if you come from an old established family in the land. But even this wears off in time.

---

1   Looming is a term found in the study of perception and occurs when an object moves closer to your eye.

2   Standing with Genesis' "In the beginning" as one of the most famous opening lines of any book of literature. Did Melville begin with this enigmatic opening to suggest a duplicitous narrator, the bastard son of Abraham, the familiarity of a commoner? It has also been suggested that Ishmael can be the orphaned son of Ahab, a retelling of an imagined version of the life of his father absent in obsessive pursuit of the Great Whale?

3   What did Melville mean by "a substitute for pistol and ball"? It has been argued that Ishmael may be referring to a life of military service, or calling someone a pistol used to have a meaning of "unpredictable", as the ball might not fly in a straight line. Or finally, and more morbidly, Ishmael may have meant suicide as an option.

4   Strong pole used for a mast.

What of it if some old hunk of a sea-captain orders me to get a broom and sweep down the decks? What does that indignity amount to, weighed, I mean, in the New Testament scales? Do you think the archangel Gabriel thinks anything the less of me because I promptly and respectfully obey that old hunk in this particular instance? Who ain't a slave? Tell me that. Well, then, however, the old sea-captains may order me about—however, they may thump and punch me about, I have the satisfaction of knowing that it is all right; that everybody else is one way or another treated in much the same way—either in a physical or metaphysical sense; and so the universal thump is passed around, and all hands should rub each other's shoulder-blades, and be content.

Again, I always go to sea as a sailor because they make a point of paying me for my trouble, whereas they never pay passengers a single penny that I ever heard of. On the contrary, passengers themselves must pay. And there is all the difference in the world between paying and being paid. The act of paying is perhaps the most uncomfortable infliction that the two orchard thieves[5] entailed upon us. But *being paid*—what compares with it?

Finally, I always go to sea as a sailor because of the wholesome exercise and pure air. For as in this world, headwinds are far more prevalent than winds from astern (that is, if you never violate the Pythagorean maxim[6]), so for the most part, the Commodore on the upper deck gets his atmosphere at second hand from the sailors on the lower. He thinks he breathes it first, but not so. In much the same way does the commonality lead their leaders in many other things, while the leaders little suspect it.

Why, after having repeatedly smelt the sea as a merchant sailor, should I now take it into my head to go on a whaling voyage? The Fates' invisible officer, who has constant surveillance of me, and secretly dogs me, and influences me—he can better answer than anyone else.

And, doubtless, my going on this whaling voyage formed part of Providence's grand program that was drawn up a long time ago. I take it that this part of the bill must have run something like this:

---

5   Reference to Adam and Eve and humankind's ever lurking debt to God.

6   This is Melville's humour surfacing early. The Pythagorean maxim is not the Pythagorean Theorem we all learned in school ($a^2 + b^2 = c^2$). The Pythagorean maxim is a rule of antiquity from the Pythagorean cult that his disciples should not eat beans due to an excess of flatulence.

"Grand Contested Election for the Presidency of the United States."
"WHALING VOYAGE BY ONE ISHMAEL. "BLOODY BATTLE IN AFGHANISTAN"[7]

Though I cannot tell why the Fates put me down for this shabby part of a whaling voyage when others were set for magnificent parts in high tragedies, I can see a little into the springs and motives which induced me to set about performing the part I did.

Chief among these motives was the overwhelming idea of the great whale himself. Such a portentous and mysterious monster roused all my curiosity. Then the wild and distant seas where he rolled; the undeliverable, nameless perils of the whale[8]; these, with all the attending marvels of a thousand Patagonian[9] sights and sounds, helped to sway me to my wish. Perhaps, with other men, such things would not have been inducements; but for me, I am tormented with an everlasting itch for things remote. I love to sail forbidden seas and land on barbarous coasts.

Because of these things, then, the whaling voyage was welcome; the great flood-gates of the wonder-world swung open, and in the wild vanity that swayed me to my purpose and floated into my inmost soul, endless processions of the whale, and, midmost of them all, one grand hooded phantom, like a snow hill in the air.

---

7   "And here we are, you and I -- not about to undertake a whaling voyage, most likely, since whaling voyages are scarce and environmentally unpopular these days, but nevertheless about to undertake some small, private voyage of our own choosing, while around us, above and below, the more extensive performances of the world loom on: a grand contested Presidential election, and some very bloody battles in Afghanistan". Roger Roseblatt - The Washington Post

8   The book was first published with the title "The Whale" before it was changed from "Mocha Dick" to "Moby Dick".

9   A tableland region of South America. The study of its indigenous inhabitants, the Tehuelche, and its unusual wildlife have attracted many scientific expeditions, including that of Charles Darwin.

Chapter 2. The Carpet-Bag[10]

Istuffed a shirt or two into my old carpet-bag, tucked it under my arm, and started for Cape Horn and the Pacific. Leaving the good city of old Manhatto[11], I duly arrived in New Bedford. It was a Saturday night in December. Much was I disappointed upon learning that the little packet[12] for Nantucket had already sailed and that there was no way of reaching that place until the following Monday.

Most young candidates for the pains and penalties of whaling stop at New Bedford, before they embark on their voyage. I, for one, chose not to. My mind was made up to sail in no other than a Nantucket craft because there was something about everything connected with that famous old island, which excited me.

Though New Bedford has gradually monopolizing the business of whaling, and the poor old Nantucket is now much behind her, yet Nantucket was her great original—the Tyre of this Carthage[13];—the place where the first dead American whale was stranded.

Now having a night, a day, and still another night in New Bedford, before I could embark for my destined port, it became a matter of concern where I was to eat and sleep.

It was a very dubious-looking, nay, a very dark and dismal night, bitingly cold and cheerless. I knew no one in the place. I had reached in my pocket with anxious grapnels[14] and only brought up a few pieces of silver. So, wherever you go, Ishmael, I said to myself, as I stood in the middle of a dreary street shouldering my bag and comparing the gloom towards the north with the darkness towards the south—wherever in your wisdom you may conclude to lodge for the night, my dear Ishmael, be sure to inquire the price and don't be too particular.

---

10   A carpet bag is a traveling bag, a suitcase of the 19th century.

11   Manhattan. Melville later uses the term "Manhattoes" to refer sarcastically (sardonically, playfully?) to people from Manhattan, the most important and elitist U.S. city at the time.

12   Packets were medium sized boats designed for domestic mail and passenger transportation.

13   Tyre was the center of the Phoenician world, serving as an economic and political hub. A port city that fueled the growth of Carthage, the "new town" blossoming into a rival to Rome.

14   The grappling hook was originally used in naval warfare to catch ship rigging so that it could be boarded. Here Ishmael is referencing his fingers, metaphorically.

I paced the streets with halting steps. Such dreary streets! Blocks of blackness, not houses. At this hour of the night, of the last day of the week, that quarter of the town proved all but deserted. I came to a smoky light proceeding from a low, wide building, the door of which stood invitingly open. So, entering, the first thing I did was to stumble over an ash-box in the porch. Ha! Thought I, ha, as the flying particles almost choked me, are these ashes from that destroyed city, Gomorrah[15]? However, I picked myself up and, hearing a loud voice within, pushed on and opened a second interior door.

It seemed the great Black Parliament was sitting in Tophet[16]. A hundred black faces turned round in their rows to peer, and beyond, a black Angel of Doom was beating a book in a pulpit. It was a black church; the preacher's text was about the blackness of darkness and the weeping and wailing and teeth-gnashing there. Ha, Ishmael, muttered I, backing out,

Moving on, I, at last, came to a dim sort of light not far from the docks, and heard a forlorn creaking in the air; and looking up, saw a swinging sign over the door with a white painting upon it, faintly representing a tall, straight jet of misty spray, and these words underneath— "The Spouter Inn:—Peter Coffin."

Coffin?—Spouter?—Rather ominous in that particular connection, I thought.

It was a queer sort of place—a gable-ended old house, one side palsied[17] as it were, and leaning over sadly. It stood on a sharp bleak corner, where that tempestuous wind Euroclydon[18] kept up a worse howling than ever it did about poor Paul's tossed craft[19].

But no more of this blubbering now, we are going a-whaling, and there is plenty of that yet to come. Let us scrape the ice from our frosted feet and see what sort of a place this "Spouter" may be.

---

15   Lot's wife, a biblical character, looked back in the past to see the destruction of Sodom and Gomorrah. She turned into a pillar of salt. (Genesis 19:26)

16   "And they have built the high places of Tophet, which is in the valley of the son of Hinnom, to burn their sons and their daughters in the fire; which I commanded them not, neither came it into my heart." (Jeremiah 7:31)

17   Past tense of palsy (paralyzed).

18   Euroclydon is a cyclonic tempestuous northeast wind which blows in the Mediterranean

19   Acts 27:14-44

Chapter 3. The Spouter-Inn

Entering that gable-shaped Spouter-Inn, you found yourself in a wide, low, straggling entry with old-fashioned wooden panelling, reminding one of the bulwarks[20] of some condemned old craft. On one side hung a very large oil painting so thoroughly blackened with smoke, and every way defaced, that it was only by diligent study and a series of systematic visits to it, and careful inquiry of the neighbors, that you could in any way arrive at an understanding of its purpose.

But what most puzzled and confounded you was a long, limber, portentous, black mass of something hovering in the center of the picture. A boggy, soggy, squitchy picture truly, enough to drive a nervous man distracted. Yet there was something unimaginably sublime about it that froze you to it, till you involuntarily took an oath with yourself to find out what that marvellous painting meant.

It's the Black Sea in a midnight gale. It's a Hyperborean[21] winter scene. It's the breaking-up of the icebound stream of Time. All of this yielded to that one portentous something in the picture's midst. *That* once found out, and all the rest were plain. Does it not bear a faint resemblance to a gigantic fish? Even the great Leviathan himself?

The artist's design seemed this: a final theory of my own, partly based upon the aggregated opinions of many aged persons with whom I conversed upon the subject. The picture represents a Cape-Horner[22] in a great hurricane.

On the opposite wall of this entry hung an array of monstrous clubs and spears. You shuddered as you gazed and wondered what monstrous cannibal and savage could ever have gone a death-harvesting with such a hacking, horrifying implement. Mixed with these were rusty old whaling lances and harpoons, all broken and deformed. Some were storied weapons. With this once long lance, now wildly bowed, did Nathan Swain[23] kill fifteen whales between a sunrise and a sunset fifty years ago?

---

20   An extension of a ship's sides above the level of the deck.

21   In Greek mythology the Hyperboreans were a race of giants who lived "beyond the North Wind".

22   A Cape Horner is a captain of a sailing ship which has sailed around Cape Horn

23   A convert to Nantucket Quakerism and according to local legend "he was once the bravest whaler out of all Nantucket and the Vineyard."

Upon entering the place, I found many young seamen gathered about a table, examining by a dim light divers specimens of *skrimshander*[24]. I sought the landlord and, telling him I needed a room, received an answer that his house was full—not a bed unoccupied. "But avast," he added, tapping his forehead, "you aint no objections to sharing a harpooneer's blanket, have ye? I s'pose you are goin' a-whalin', so you'd better get used to that sort of thing."

I told him that I never liked to sleep two in a bed; that if I should ever do so, it would depend upon who the harpooneer might be, and that if he (the landlord) really had no other place for me, and the harpooneer was not decidedly objectionable, I would put up with the half of any decent man's blanket.

"I thought so. All right; take a seat. Supper?—you want supper? Supper'll be ready directly."

At last, some four or five of us were summoned to our meal in an adjoining room. It was cold as Iceland—no fire at all—the landlord said he couldn't afford it. But the fare was of the most substantial kind—not only meat and potatoes but dumplings; good heavens! Dumplings for supper!

"My boy," said the landlord, "you'll have the nightmare to a dead sartainty," said he, looking a sort of diabolically funny, "the harpooneer is a dark-complexioned chap. He never eats dumplings, he don't—he eats nothing but steaks, and he likes 'em rare."

"The devil he does," says I. "Where is that harpooneer? Is he here?"

"He'll be here before long," was the answer.

I could not help it, but I began to feel suspicious of this "dark-complexioned" harpooneer. At any rate, I made up my mind that if it so turned out that we should sleep together, he must undress and get into bed before I did.

The more I pondered over this harpooneer, the more I abhorred the thought of sleeping with him. Besides, it was getting late, and my decent harpooneer ought to be home and going to bed.

---

24   Handicrafts practiced by sailors by way of pastime during long whaling and other voyages such as carvings on bone, ivory, or shells.

"Landlord! I've changed my mind about that harpooneer.—I won't sleep with him. I'll try the bench here."

"Just as you please; I'm sorry I can't spare ye a tablecloth for a mattress, and it's a rough board here"—feeling of the knots and notches.

I now measured the bench and found that it was a foot too short, but that could be mended with a chair. But it was a foot too narrow, and the other bench in the room was about four inches higher—so there was no connecting them.

The devil fetch that harpooneer, thought I.

Looking round me again and seeing no possible chance of spending a sufferable night unless, in some other person's bed, I began to think that after all, I might be holding unwarranted prejudices against this unknown harpooneer. I'll wait awhile, I thought, he must be dropping in before long. I'll have a good look at him then, and perhaps we may become jolly good bedfellows after all.

But though the other boarders kept coming in by ones, twos, and threes, and going to bed, yet still no sign of my harpooneer.

"Landlord!" I asked, "what sort of a chap is he—does he always keep such late hours?" It was now close to twelve o'clock.

The landlord chuckled again with his lean chuckle and seemed to be mightily tickled at something beyond my comprehension. "No," he answered, "generally he's an early bird—airley to bed and airley to rise—yes, he's the bird what catches the worm. But tonight he went out a peddling, you see, and I don't see what on airth keeps him so late, unless, maybe, he can't sell his head."

"Can't sell his head?—What sort of a bamboozingly story is this you are telling me?" getting into a towering rage. "Do you pretend to say, landlord, that this harpooneer is actually engaged this blessed Saturday night, or rather Sunday morning, in peddling his head around this town?"

"That's precisely it," said the landlord, "and I told him he couldn't sell it here. The market's overstocked."

"With what?" I shouted.

"With heads to be sure; ain't there too many heads in the world?"

"I tell you what it is, landlord," said I quite calmly, "you'd better stop spinning that yarn to me—I'm not green."

"Maybe not," taking out a stick and whittling a toothpick, "but I rather guess you'll be done *brown*[25] if that harpooneer hears you a slanderin' his head."

"I'll break it for him," I said, now flying into a passion again at this unaccountable mythical character of the landlord's.

"It's broke a'ready," he said.

"Broke," said I—"*broke*, do you mean?"

"And that's the very reason he can't sell it, I guess."

"Landlord," I said, going up to him as cool as Mt. Hecla[26] in a snow-storm—"landlord, you and I must understand one another. I came to your house and wanted a bed; you tell me you can only give me half a one; that the other half belongs to a certain harpooneer. Then you persist in telling me the most mystifying and exasperating stories about the man who is to be my bedfellow. I now demand of you to speak out and tell me who and what this harpooneer is and whether I will be safe to spend the night with him. I have no intention of sleeping with a madman."

"Wall," said the landlord, fetching a long breath, "that's a purty long sermon for a chap that rips a little now and then. But be easy, be easy, this here harpooneer I have been tellin' you of has just arrived from the south seas, where he bought up a lot of 'balmed New Zealand heads (great ornaments, you know). He's sold all on 'em but one, and that one he's trying to sell to-night, cause to-morrow's Sunday, and it would not do to be sellin' human heads about the streets when folks are goin' to churches. He wanted to, last Sunday, but I stopped

---

25   A phrase in cookery; applied figuratively to one who has been thoroughly deceived, cheated, or fooled.

26   Mt. Hecla is an active volcano in southern Iceland. During the middle ages, Europeans called it "The Gateway to Hell".

him just as he was goin' out of the door with four heads strung on a string, for all the airth like a string of inions[27]."

This account cleared up the otherwise unaccountable mystery. It showed that the landlord, after all, had no idea of fooling me—but at the same time, what could I think of a harpooneer who stayed out on a Saturday night clean into the holy Sabbath, engaging in such a cannibal business as selling the heads of dead idolaters?

"Landlord, that harpooneer is a dangerous man." "He pays reg'lar," was the response. "But come, it's getting dreadful late, you had better be turning flukes[28]—it's a nice bed;

I considered the matter a moment, and then upstairs we went, and I was ushered into a small room, cold as a clam, and furnished, sure enough, with a bed, almost big enough indeed for any four harpooneers to sleep side by side.

"There," said the landlord, placing the candle on a crazy old sea chest that did double duty as a wash-stand and center table; "there, make yourself comfortable now, and good night to ye." I turned round from eyeing the bed, but he had disappeared.

I sat down on the side of the bed and commenced thinking about this head-peddling harpooneer. But beginning to feel very cold now, half undressed as I was, and remembering what the landlord said about the harpooneer's not coming home at all that night. It being so very late, I made no more ado, but jumped out of my pants and boots, and then blowing out the light, tumbled into bed and commended myself to the care of heaven[29].

Whether that mattress was stuffed with corn-cobs or broken dishes, there is no telling, but I rolled about a good deal and could not sleep for a long time. At last, I slid off into a light doze and had pretty nearly made off towards the land of Nod[30] when I heard heavy footsteps in the passage and saw a glimmer of light come into the room from under the door.

---

27   Onions.

28   (nautical slang) To turn in, go to bed.

29   Luke 23:46: "Father into thy hands I commend my spirit".

30   The Land of Nod is a mythical play of the term to "nod off." The Land of Nod is a place mentioned in Genesis located on the east of Eden and where Cain was exiled to after killing his brother Abel.

Lord save me, that must be the harpooneer, the infernal head-peddler. But, I lay perfectly still and resolved not to say a word till spoken to. Holding a light in one hand, and that identical New Zealand head in the other, the stranger entered the room, and without looking towards the bed, placed his candle a good way off from me on the floor in one corner, and then began working away at the knotted cords of his large bag.

He turned round—when, good heavens! What a sight! Such a face! It was of a dark, purplish, yellow color, with large blackish-looking squares. Yes, it's just as I thought, he's a terrible bedfellow; he's been in a fight, got dreadfully cut, and here he is, just from the surgeon. But at that moment, he chanced to turn his face so towards the light that I plainly saw they could not be sticking-plasters[31] at all, those black squares on his cheeks. They were stains of some sort or other.

At first, I knew not what to make of this; but soon, an inkling of the truth occurred. I remembered a story of a white man—a whaleman too—who, falling among the cannibals, had been tattooed by them. I concluded that this harpooneer must have met with a similar adventure in the course of his distant voyages.

And after all, it's only his outside; a man can be honest in any sort of skin.

He now took off his hat, a new beaver hat, and to my surprise, there was no hair on his head, none to speak of at least, nothing but a small scalp-knot twisted upon his forehead.

Had not the stranger stood between me and the door, I would have bolted out of it quicker than ever I bolted a dinner.

Even as it was, I thought something of slipping out of the window, but it was the second floor. I am no coward. Ignorance is the parent of fear, and being completely confounded by the stranger, I confess I was now as much afraid of him as if it was the devil himself who had broken into my room at the dead of night. I was so afraid of him that I was not brave enough to address him.

Meanwhile, he continued the business of undressing and, at last, showed his chest and arms. As I live, these covered parts of him were checkered with the same squares as his face;

---

31   An adhesive bandage used in dressing wounds.

his back, too, was all over the same dark squares; he seemed to have been in a Thirty Years' War[32] and just escaped from it with a bandage for a shirt.

It was now quite plain that he must be some abominable savage shipped aboard a whaleman in the South Seas and landed in this Christian country. I quaked[33] to think of it. A peddler of heads too—perhaps the heads of his brothers. He might take a fancy to mine—heavens! Look at that tomahawk!

But there was no time for shuddering, for now, the savage went about something that completely fascinated my attention and convinced me that he must indeed be a heathen.

Going to his heavy coat, which he had previously hung on a chair, he fumbled in the pockets and produced at length a curious little deformed black manikin. I concluded that it must be nothing but a wooden idol, which indeed it proved to be.

The Savage walked to the empty fireplace and set up this little hunch-backed image, like a tenpin[34], between the log supports. This fire-place made a very appropriate little shrine or chapel for his Congo idol.

Next, he took about a double handful of shavings out of his coat pocket, and placed them carefully before the idol; then, laying crumbs of a biscuit on top and applying the flame from the lamp, he kindled the shavings into a sacrificial blaze and he made a polite offer of it to the little idol. All these strange antics were accompanied by still stranger guttural noises from the devotee, who seemed to be praying in a sing-song or else singing some pagan psalm, during which his face twitched about in the most unnatural manner.

All of this increased my discomfort especially seeing that he was getting ready to jump into bed with me. I thought it was high time, now or never, before the light was put out, to break the spell in which I had so long been bound.

---

32   The Thirty Years War was a religious conflict started in Europe by an attempt of the King of Bohemia to impose Catholicism throughout his kingdoms. The Protestants rebelled. The war remains one of the longest and most brutal wars in human history with up to 60% death in some German populations.

33   A reference to the religion of Nantucket. To quake at the name of God.

34   A wooden pin used in ten-pin bowling.

But the interval I spent in deliberating what to say, was a fatal one. Taking up his tomahawk from the table, he examined the head of it for an instant, and then holding it to the light, he puffed out great clouds of tobacco smoke. The next moment the light was extinguished, and this wild cannibal, tomahawk between his teeth, sprang into bed with me. I sang out, I could not help it now, and gave a sudden grunt of astonishment.

"Who the devil are you?"—he, at last, said—"you don't speak, I'll kill you."

"Landlord, for God's sake, Peter Coffin!" shouted I. "Landlord! Coffin! Angels! Save me!"

"Speak! Tell me who you be, or dam-me, I kill ye!" again growled the cannibal while his horrid flourishings of the tomahawk scattered the hot tobacco ashes about me till I thought my linen would get on fire. But thank heaven, at that moment the landlord came into the room light in hand and leaping from the bed, I ran up to him.

"Don't be afraid now," said he, grinning again, "Queequeg here wouldn't harm a hair of your head." "Stop your grinning," I shouted, "and why didn't you tell me that infernal harpooneer was a cannibal?"

"I thought ye knew it;—didn't I tell ye, he was a peddlin' heads around town? Queequeg, look here—you understand me, this man sleep with you—you understand?" "Me understand plenty"—grunted Queequeg, puffing away at his pipe and sitting up in bed.

"You gettee in," he added, motioning to me with his tomahawk, and throwing the clothes to one side. He really did this in not only a civil but a really kind and charitable way. I stood looking at him a moment. For all his tattooings, he was, on the whole, a clean, comely looking cannibal. What's all this fuss I have been making about, thought I to myself—the man's a human being just as I am: he has just as much reason to fear me as I have to be afraid of him. Better sleep with a sober cannibal than a drunken Christian.[35]

"Good night, landlord," said I, "you may go." I turned in and never slept better in my life.

---

35   This line by Melville is certainly one of the most discussed from the novel. One interpretation is that a "drunken Christian" means a religious zealot so blinded by their certainties of right vs wrong that they can harm others or themselves with their dogma, bigotry and judgment. And Cannibals aren't likely to eat their friends, especially when in their right mind. An alternative explanation is that alcohol depresses the central nervous system affecting the portion of the brain that keeps your mouth, nose and throat muscles open. Snoring results.

Chapter 4. The Counterpane[36]

Upon waking the next morning about daylight, I found Queequeg's arm thrown over me in the most loving and affectionate manner. You had almost thought I had been his wife. The counterpane was of patchwork, full of odd little colored squares and triangles; and this arm of his tattooed all over with endless Cretan labyrinth[37] figures, no two parts of which were of one precise shade—owing I suppose to his keeping his arm at sea unmethodically in the sun and shade, his shirt sleeves irregularly rolled up at various times.

My sensations were strange. Let me try to explain them.

When I was a child, I well remember a somewhat similar circumstance; whether it was a reality or a dream, I never could entirely settle. This is what I remember. I think I was trying to crawl up the chimney, as I had seen a little sweep do a few days previously; and my stepmother, who was all the time whipping me, or sending me to bed supperless, dragged me by the legs out of the chimney and packed me off to bed, though it was only two o'clock in the afternoon of the 21st June, the longest day in the year in our hemisphere. I felt dreadful. But there was no help for it, so up the stairs, I went to my little room on the third floor, undressed as slowly as possible so as to kill time, and with a bitter sigh got in bed.

I lay there dismally calculating that sixteen entire hours must elapse before I could hope for a resurrection. Sixteen hours in bed! The small of my back ached to think of it. And it was so light too; the sun shining in at the window, and a great rattling of coaches in the streets, and the sound of voices all over the house. I felt worse and worse—at last, I got up, dressed, and softly going down in my stockinged feet, sought out my stepmother, and suddenly threw myself at her feet, begging her as a particular favor to give me a good whipping for my misbehavior; anything indeed but condemning me to lie in bed for such an unendurable length of time. But she was the best and most conscientious of stepmothers, and back I had to go to my room. For several hours I lay there wide awake, feeling a great deal worse than I have ever felt since. At last, I must have fallen into a troubled nightmare of a doze, and slowly waking from it—half steeped in dreams—I opened my eyes, and the before sun-

---

36 Bedspread.

37 Greek Island maze type structures.

lit room was now wrapped in outer darkness. Instantly I felt a shock running through all my frame; nothing was to be seen, and nothing was to be heard, but a supernatural hand seemed placed in mine. My arm hung over my bed, and the nameless, unimaginable, silent form or phantom, to which the hand belonged, seemed closely seated by my bed-side. For what seemed ages piled on ages, I lay there, frozen with the most awful fears, not daring to drag away my hand, yet ever thinking that if I could but stir it one single inch, the horrid spell would be broken. I knew not how this consciousness, at last, left me. Still, waking in the morning, I shudderingly remembered it all, and for days and weeks and months afterward, I lost myself in confounding attempts to explain the mystery.

Yes, to this very hour, I often puzzle myself with it.[38]

Now, take away the awful fear, and my sensations at feeling the supernatural hand in mine were very similar, in their strangeness, to those which I experienced on waking up and seeing Queequeg's pagan arm thrown around me.

Yet, sleeping as he was, he still hugged me tightly, as though only death should part us. I now strove to rouse him—"Queequeg!"—but his only answer was a snore. A pretty pickle, truly, thought I; in bed here in a strange house in the broad day, with a cannibal and a tomahawk!

"Queequeg!—in the name of goodness, Queequeg, wake!"

He drew back his arm, shook himself all over like a Newfoundland dog just from the water, and sat up in bed, looking at me, and rubbing his eyes as if he did not altogether remember how I came to be there. When, at last, he jumped out upon the floor, and by certain signs and sounds explained that he would dress first and then leave me to dress afterward, leaving the whole apartment to myself. I thought that under the circumstances, this was a very civilized overture; but, the truth is, these savages have an innate sense of delicacy, say what you will; it is marvelous how essentially polite they are. I pay this particular compliment to Queequeg because he treated me with so much civility while I was guilty of great rudeness.

A man like Queequeg you don't see every day, he and his ways were well worth regarding.

---

38   As seen in the opening four chapters, Ishmael refuses to proclaim his religion above any others, preferring to retain a sceptical, universal religious worldview. However, we also see that Ishmael, much like the author who created him, was still energized by the mystery of the universe and the Hand of Providence that he recognizes as an influence in his life.

Chapter 5. Breakfast

I quickly descended into the bar-room which was now full of the boarders who had been dropping in the previous night. They were nearly all whalemen; chief mates, second mates, third mates, sea carpenters, sea coopers, sea blacksmiths, harpooneers, and ship keepers; a brown and brawny company, with bosky[39] beards; all wearing monkey jackets[40] for morning gowns.

[41]

You could pretty plainly tell how long each one had been ashore.

---

39 Wooded; covered by trees or bushes.

40 Historically monkey jackets were commonly worn by sailors. This style of jacket was named after the ones worn by monkeys that accompanied organ grinders.

41 A sailor wearing a monkey jacket.

"Grub, ho!" now cried the landlord, flinging open a door, and in we went to breakfast.

I was preparing to hear some good stories about whaling; however, to my surprise, nearly every man maintained a profound silence. And not only that, but they looked shy. Yes, here were a set of sea-dogs, many of whom without the slightest bashfulness had boarded great whales on the high seas and dueled them dead without winking; and yet, here they sat at a social breakfast table—all of the same calling, all of kindred tastes—looking round sheepishly at each other. A curious sight; these bashful bears, these timid warrior whalemen![42]

But as for Queequeg—why, Queequeg sat there among them—at the head of the table, as cool as an icicle. His greatest admirer could not have justified his bringing his harpoon into breakfast with him, and reaching over the table with it, to the imminent jeopardy of many heads, and grappling the beefsteaks towards him. But *that* was certainly very coolly done by him, and everyone knows that in most people's estimation, to do anything coolly is to do it gracefully.

We will not speak of all Queequeg's peculiarities here; how he eschewed coffee and hot rolls and applied his undivided attention to beefsteaks, done rare. Enough that when breakfast was over, he withdrew like the rest into the public room, lighted his tomahawk-pipe, and was sitting there quietly digesting and smoking with his inseparable hat on when I sallied out for a stroll.

---

42   Though Melville seemingly makes a dig at these roughened and fearless "sea-dogs" for not having enough courage to hold a conversation (bashful bears), he also subtly respects this about them. In Melville's Journals, of which he allowed very little to be preserved, he recalls a dinner he attended with an elitist highbrow who was "full of himself and expected great homage" and Melville abstained from conversation. "I refrained from playing the snob to him, like the rest." *Journals Friday Nov 3, 1984.*

Chapter 6. The Street

If I had been astonished at so outlandish an individual as Queequeg among the polite society of a civilized town, that astonishment soon departed upon taking my first daylight stroll through the streets of New Bedford.

But New Bedford beats all Water Street[43] and Wapping[44]. In these places, you see only sailors; but in New Bedford, actual cannibals stand chatting at street corners, savages outright. And the women of New Bedford, they bloom like their own red roses. Where roses only bloom in summer, theirs is perennial. Elsewhere match that bloom of theirs? Ye cannot.

The town itself is perhaps the dearest place to live in, in all New England. It is a land of oil, true enough: but not like Canaan[45]; a land, also, of corn and wine. Nowhere in all America will you find more patrician[46]-like houses; parks, and gardens more opulent than in New Bedford. Where did it come from? How did all of this grow among this refuse of a country?

Go and gaze upon the emblematical harpoons around lofty mansion, and your question will be answered. Yes, all these brave houses and flowery gardens came from the Atlantic, Pacific, and Indian oceans. One and all, they were harpooned and dragged up hither from the bottom of the sea. Can Herr Alexander[47] perform a feat like that?

---

43   Water Street is one of Liverpool's oldest streets and it was the main approach from the river. Melville arrived in Liverpool when he was 19 years old, not as a whaler, but a greenhorn sailor on a merchant ship. His time spent here was memorable enough that it was the basis for his novel *Redburn.*

44   Wapping is a district in East London. It is situated between the north bank of the River Thames and the ancient thoroughfare simply called The Highway. Wapping's proximity to the river has given it a strong maritime character. Melville came to London two years before he published Moby Dick. In his diary, he recorded seeing the Lord Mayor's Show, a public hanging, the British Museum, the National Gallery and London Zoo. He was a curious sightseer.

45   The land promised to Moses in the bible. A land of "milk and honey". (Exodus 3:17).

46   Patricians were rich Roman landowners who lived in expensive homes called domus. A domus was an expensive, fancy, and often a very large house. The modern word "domestic" (which means "relating to the home") comes from the same root word "domus" comes from.

47   Confused by some people to be a reference to Alexander the Great. This Herr Alexander was most certainly a reference to Johann Friedrich Alexander Heimburgher, a popular but long forgotten German magician of the time. The "David Copperfield" of the early 19th century.

Chapter 7. The Chapel

In this same New Bedford, there stands a Whaleman's Chapel, and few are the fishermen, soon bound for the Indian Ocean or Pacific, who fail to make a Sunday visit to the spot. I am sure that I did not.

The sky had changed from clear, sunny cold to driving sleet and mist. Wrapping myself in my shaggy jacket, I fought my way against the stubborn storm. Entering, I found a small scattered congregation of sailors and sailors' wives and widows. A muffled silence reigned, only broken at times by the shrieks of the storm. Each silent worshipper seemed purposely sitting apart from the other as if each silent grief were insular and incommunicable. The chaplain had not yet arrived, and there these silent islands of men and women sat steadfastly eyeing several marble tablets, with black borders, masoned into the wall on either side of the pulpit. Three of them ran something like the following, but I do not pretend to quote:—

SACRED TO THE MEMORY OF JOHN TALBOT, who was lost overboard at the age of eighteen, Near the Isle of Desolation, off Patagonia, *November 1st*, 1836. THIS TABLET Is erected to his Memory BY HIS SISTER.

SACRED TO THE MEMORY OF ROBERT LONG, WILLIS ELLERY, NATHAN COLEMAN, WALTER CANNY, SETH MACY, AND SAMUEL GLEIG, Forming one of the boats' crews OF THE SHIP ELIZA Who were towed out of sight by a Whale, On the Off-shore Ground in the PACIFIC, *December 31st*, 1839. Their surviving SHIPMATES place THIS MARBLE.

SACRED TO THE MEMORY OF The late CAPTAIN EZEKIEL HARDY, Who in the bows of his boat was killed by a Sperm Whale on the coast of Japan, *August 3d*, 1833. THIS TABLET Is erected to his Memory BY HIS WIDOW.

Shaking off the sleet from my ice-glazed hat and jacket, I seated myself near the door, and turning sideways, was surprised to see Queequeg near me. Affected by the solemnity of the scene, there was a wondering gaze of incredulous curiosity in his countenance. This savage was the only person present who seemed to notice my entrance; because he was the only one who could not read and, therefore, was not reading those frigid inscriptions on the wall. Whether any of the relatives of the seamen whose names appeared there were now among the congregation, I knew not; but so many are the unrecorded accidents in the fishery, and so plainly did several women present wear the countenance of some unceasing grief, that I feel sure that here before me were assembled those, in whose unhealing hearts the sight of these bleak tablets sympathetically caused the old wounds to bleed afresh.

But Faith, like a jackal, feeds among the tombs, and even from these dead doubts, she gathers her most vital hope.[48]

It needs scarcely to be told, with what feelings, on the eve of a Nantucket voyage, I regarded those marble tablets[49], and by the murky light of that darkened, doleful day read the fate of the whalemen who had gone before me. Yes, Ishmael, the same fate may be thine. But somehow, I grew merry again.

I think we have hugely mistaken this matter of Life and Death. I think that what they call my shadow[50] here on earth is my true substance. I think that in looking at things spiritual, we are too much like oysters[51] observing the sun through the water and thinking that thick water the thinnest of air. In fact, take my body, it is not me. And therefore, three cheers for Nantucket; and come a stove boat[52] and stove body when they will, for stave my soul, Jove[53] himself cannot.

---

48   Faith finds nourishment in contemplation of death. When Herman Melville was 12 years old his father Allan Melville died. Allan subscribed to Unitarianism (recognizing the inherent worth of every human being and supporting everyone's search for meaning), while Herman's mother was a strict Calvinist and created a family culture that was strictly puritanistic; likely causing a friction between Herman and religion.

49   Exodus 31: 18: When the Lord finished speaking to Moses on Mount Sinai, he gave him the two tablets of the covenant law, the tablets of stone inscribed by the finger of God.

50   Soul.

51   Likely a reference to Paul's pronouncement in 1 Corinthians 13:12: "For now we see through a glass, darkly; but then face to face."

52   Stove is the past tense of stave which is an old whaling term to smash a hole into something. Stove was often a reference to the mighty slapping of a harpooned whale's tail coming down onto a fragile boat.

53   Jove, in Roman mythology, is the king of the gods and the god of sky and thunder, equivalent to Zeus in Greek traditions. This final sentence of Chapter 7 could simply read, "You can destroy my body, but not my soul."

Chapter 8. The Pulpit

I had not been seated very long when a man of certain venerable[54] robustness entered; a quick scan of him by the congregation sufficiently attested that this fine old man was the chaplain. Yes, it was the famous Father Mapple, so-called by the whalemen, among whom he was a very great favorite. He had been a sailor and a harpooneer in his youth, but he had dedicated his life to the ministry for many years. At the time I now write of, Father Mapple was in the hardy winter of a healthy old age; that sort of old age which seems to merge into a second flowering youth, for among all the fissures of his wrinkles, there shone certain mild gleams of a newly developing bloom—spring vegetation peeping forth even beneath February's snow.

No one, having previously heard his history, could for the first time behold Father Mapple without the utmost interest because there were certain clerical peculiarities about him related to that adventurous maritime life he had led.

When he entered, I observed that he carried no umbrella and certainly had not come in his carriage, for his hat ran down with melting sleet, and his great pilot cloth jacket seemed almost to drag him to the floor with the weight of the water it had absorbed. However, hat and coat and overshoes were one by one removed and hung up in a little space in an adjacent corner; when arrayed in a decent order, he quietly approached the pulpit.

Like most old fashioned pulpits, it was a very lofty one, the architect, it seemed, had acted upon the hint of Father Mapple, and finished the pulpit without stairs, substituting a perpendicular side ladder, like those used in mounting a ship from a boat at sea. Father Mapple cast a look upwards, and then with a truly sailor-like but still reverential dexterity, hand over hand, mounted the steps as if ascending the main-top of his vessel.

I was not prepared to see Father Mapple after gaining the height, slowly turning around, and stooping over the pulpit, deliberately dragging up the ladder step by step, till the whole was deposited within, leaving him impregnable in his little Quebec[55].

---

54   Accorded a great deal of respect, especially because of age, wisdom, or character

55   A reference to Citadlle de Quebec, a fortress city built by the French with high slopes defending its sides from invasion.

I pondered some time without fully comprehending the reason for this. Father Mapple enjoyed such a wide reputation for sincerity and sanctity that I could not suspect him of courting notoriety by any mere tricks of the stage. No, thought I, there must be some sober reason for this thing; furthermore, it must symbolize something unseen. Can it be, then, that he signifies his spiritual withdrawal for the time from all outward worldly ties and connections by that act of physical isolation? Yes, for replenished with the meat and wine[56] of the word, to the faithful man of God, this pulpit, I see, is a self-containing stronghold—a lofty Ehrenbreitstein[57], with a perennial well[58] of water within the walls.

On both sides of the pulpit, the wall was adorned with a large painting representing a gallant ship beating against a terrible storm off a lee coast[59]. But high above the flying scud[60] and dark-rolling clouds, there floated a little isle of sunlight, from which beamed forth an angel's face; and this bright face shed a distinct spot of radiance upon the ship's tossed deck, something like that silver plate now inserted into the Victory's plank where Nelson[61] fell. "Ah, noble ship," the angel seemed to say, "beat on, beat on, thou noble ship, for lo! the sun is breaking through; the clouds are rolling off—serenity is at hand."

The pulpit itself was paneled in the likeness of a ship's bows, and the Holy Bible rested on the ship's fiddle-headed beak.[62]

What could be more full of meaning?—for the pulpit is ever this earth's foremost part; all the rest comes in its rear; the pulpit leads the world. From then, it is the storm of God's quick wrath, and the bow must bear the earliest brunt. Yes, the world's a ship on its passage out, and not a voyage complete, and the pulpit is its bow.

---

56   Isaiah 25:6 - On this mountain the LORD Almighty will prepare a feast of rich food for all peoples, a banquet of aged wine-- the best of meats and the finest of wines.

57   A fortress in Germany besieged by French Revolutionary troops three times in 1794, unsuccessfully.

58   John 4: 6-14.

59   A stretch of shoreline that is to the lee side of a vessel —meaning the wind is blowing towards it.

60   The goal of scud sailing is to stay clear of the weather.

61   Horatio Nelson was the most famous admiral of the Napoleonic Wars who has been celebrated ever since as the greatest sea warrior in British history. He died in the Battle of Trafalgar, the greatest of British navy battles and his last words were "Thank God I have done my duty." The name of his ship was Victory.

62   The Seamen's Bethel is a real Chapel in New Bedford Built by the *New Bedford Port Society*, it was completed on May 2, 1832 fitted with the immortalized bow-shaped pulpit, seemingly shaped as a cross.

Chapter 9. The Sermon

Father Mapple rose, and in a mild voice of unassuming authority, ordered the scattered people to condense. "Starboard gangway, there! Side away to larboard—larboard gangway to starboard! Midships! Midships!"

There was a low rumbling of heavy sea-boots among the benches and a still slighter shuffling of women's shoes, and all was quiet again, and every eye on the preacher.

He paused a little; then, kneeling in the pulpit's bows, folded his large brown hands across his chest, uplifted his closed eyes, and offered a prayer so deeply devout that he seemed kneeling and praying at the bottom of the sea.

This ended, in prolonged solemn tones, like the continual tolling of a bell in a ship that is foundering at sea in a fog—in such tones he commenced reading the following hymn; but changing his manner towards the concluding stanzas, burst forth with a pealing[63] exultation and joy:

In black distress, I called my God,
When I could scarce believe him mine,
He bowed his ear to my complaints—
No more the whale did me confine.

With speed, he flew to my relief,
As on a radiant dolphin borne;
Awful, yet bright, as lightning shone
The face of my Deliverer God.

---

63   Melville was acquainted with Henry Longfellow living near each other in Massachusetts and maybe a little jealous of his success as a poet, while he was a bankrupted author of unsellable books. The sermon of Father Mapple draws similarities to Longfellow's "I heard the Bells on Christmas Day", written in 1863, thirteen years after Moby Dick was released. "Then pealed the bells more loud and deep: God is not dead, nor doth He sleep." Longfellow notes in his journal: "Sat to read all the evening in Melville's new book Moby Dick or the Whale, very wild, strange and interesting."

My song forever shall record
That terrible, that joyful hour;
I give the glory to my God,
His all the mercy and the power."

Nearly all joined in singing this hymn, which swelled high above the howling of the storm. A brief pause ensued; the preacher slowly turned over the leaves of the Bible, and at last, folding his hand down upon the proper page, said: "Beloved shipmates, clinch the last verse of the first chapter of Jonah—'And God had prepared a great fish to swallow up Jonah.'"

"Shipmates, this book, containing only four chapters—four yarns—is one of the smallest strands in the mighty cable of the Scriptures. Yet what depths of the soul does Jonah's deep sealine sound! What a pregnant lesson to us is this prophet! What a noble thing is that canticle[64] in the fish's belly! How billow-like and boisterously grand! We feel the floods surging over us! But *what* is this lesson that the book of Jonah teaches? Shipmates, it is a two-stranded lesson, a lesson to us all, and a lesson to me as a pilot of the living God.

As sinful men, it is a lesson to us all because it is a story of sin, hard-heartedness, suddenly awakened fears, the swift punishment, repentance, prayers, and finally, the deliverance and joy of Jonah. As with all sinners among men, the sin of this son of Amittai[65] was in his wilful disobedience of the command of God, which he found a hard command. But all the things that God would have us do are hard for us to do—remember that—and hence, he more often commands us than endeavors to persuade. And if we obey God, we must disobey ourselves.

"With this sin of disobedience in him, Jonah still further flouts at God by seeking to flee from Him. He thinks that a ship made by men will carry him into countries where God does not reign. He skulks[66] about the wharf of Joppa and seeks a ship that's bound for Tarshish. There lurks, perhaps, a previously ignored meaning here.

See ye not, shipmates, that Jonah sought to flee world-wide from God?

---

64   A hymn or a chant.

65   Amittai is only mentioned twice in the Bible, in 2 Kings 14:25 and Jonah 1:1. Nothing is known about him, other than that he was Jonah's father.

66   To move in a stealthy manner.

There now came a lull in his look, as he silently turned over the leaves of the Book once more; and, at last, standing motionless, with closed eyes, for the moment, seemed to commune with God himself.

But again he leaned over towards the people and bowing his head lowly, with an aspect of the deepest yet manliest humility, he spake these words:

"Shipmates, God has laid but one hand upon you; both his hands press upon me. I have read ye the lesson that Jonah teaches to all sinners; and therefore to ye, and still more to me, for I am a greater sinner than ye. And now how gladly would I come down from this mast-head and sit on the hatches there where you sit, and listen as you listen, while one of you read to me that other and more awful lesson which Jonah teaches to *me*, as a pilot of the living God. How being an anointed pilot-prophet, or speaker of true things, and bidden by the Lord to sound those unwelcome truths in the ears of a wicked Nineveh, Jonah, appalled at the hostility he should raise, fled from his mission and sought to escape his duty and his God by taking ship at Joppa. But God is everywhere; Tarshish he never reached. As we have seen, God came upon him in the whale and swallowed him down to living gulfs of doom.

Yet even then, beyond the reach of any plummet—'out of the belly of hell'—when the whale grounded upon the ocean's utmost bones, even then, God heard the engulfed, repenting prophet when he cried. Then God spake unto the fish; and from the shuddering cold and blackness of the sea, the whale came breeching up towards the warm and pleasant sun, and all the delights of air and earth; and 'vomited out Jonah upon the dry land. When the word of the Lord came a second time, and Jonah, bruised and beaten—did the Almighty's bidding. And what was that, shipmates? To preach the Truth to the face of Falsehood! That was it!"

He dropped and fell away from himself for a moment; then lifting his face to them again, showed a deep joy in his eyes, as he cried out with a heavenly enthusiasm,—"But oh! shipmates! on the starboard hand of every woe, there is a sure delight; And eternal delight and deliciousness will be his, who coming to lay him down, can say with his final breath—O Father!— here I die. I have striven to be Thine, more than to be this world's, or my own."

He said no more, but slowly offering a benediction, covered his face with his hands, and so remained kneeling till all the people had departed, and he was left alone in the place.

Chapter 10. A Bosom Friend

Returning to the Spouter-Inn from the Chapel, I found Queequeg there quite alone; he having left the Chapel sometime before the benediction. He was sitting on a bench before the fire, and in one hand was holding close up to his face that little black idol of his; peering hard into its face, and with a jack-knife gently whittling away at its nose, meanwhile humming to himself in his heathen-ish way.

But being now interrupted, he put up the image; and pretty soon, going to the table, took up a large book there, and placing it on his lap, began counting the pages with deliberate regularity; at every fiftieth page. He would then begin again at the next fifty, seeming to commence at number one each time, as though he could not count more than fifty, and it was only by such a large number of fifties being found together that his astonishment at the multitude of pages was excited.

With much interest,[67] I sat watching him. Savage though he was, and hideously marred about the face—at least to my taste—his countenance yet had a something in it which was by no means disagreeable. You cannot hide the soul.

Through all his unearthly tattooings, I thought I saw the traces of a simple, honest heart; and in his large, deep eyes, fiery black and bold, there seemed tokens of a spirit that would dare a thousand devils.

Whether it was that his head being shaved, his forehead looked more expansive than it otherwise would, this I will not venture to decide; but certain it was. His head was phrenologically[68] an excellent one. It may seem ridiculous, but it reminded me of General Washington's head, as seen in the popular busts of him.

---

67   Even before Tik Tok, Instagram and Facebook, Melville understood the "look at me culture" and shunned it. How content is Queequeg to find a hobby, even mundane as counting pages of a book, without anyone watching? Enjoying a task for its own sake without feeling the need to show it off to the world for confirmation.

68   The study of the conformation and especially the contours of the skull based on the former belief that they are indicative of mental faculties and character.

Queequeg was George Washington[69] cannibalistically developed.

While I was thus closely scanning him, half-pretending meanwhile to be looking out at the storm from the window, he never heeded my presence, never troubled himself with so much as a single glance; but appeared wholly occupied with counting the pages of the marvelous book.

I had also noticed that Queequeg never mingled at all, or but very little, with the other seamen in the inn. He made no advances whatsoever; he appeared to have no desire to enlarge the circle of his acquaintances. All this struck me as remarkable; yet, upon second thought, there was something almost sublime in it. Here was a man some twenty thousand miles from home, thrown among people as strange to him as though he were in the planet Jupiter, and yet he seemed entirely at his ease; preserving the utmost serenity; content with his own companionship; always equal to himself.

Surely this was a touch of fine philosophy, though no doubt he had never heard there was such a thing as that. But, perhaps, to be true philosophers, we mortals should not be conscious of so living or so striving. So as soon as I hear that such or such a man gives himself out for a philosopher, I conclude that, like the dyspeptic old woman, he must have "broken his digester."[70]

As I sat there in that now lonely room; the fire burning low; I began to be sensible of strange feelings. I felt a melting in me. No more, my splintered heart and maddened hand were turned against the wolfish world. This soothing savage had redeemed it.

There he sat, his very indifference speaking a nature in which there lurked no civilized hypocrisies and bland deceits. Wild he was; a very sight of sights to see, yet I began to feel mysteriously drawn towards him. And those same things that would have repelled

---

69   As Melville burned most of his writings, it is very rare to find anything penned by him. However, there was a recent auction of one of his letters to a friend, and attorney, Kenney Furlong Esq. The letter read in part: *"Many thanks for your enclosed etching of Washington's head."* This is believed to be a sarcastic reference to a 10 cent stamp bearing George Washington's bust that was the postage for the letter. The letter sold for $4,000.

70   A digester was a machine, a pressure cooker. It would take a lot of steam, or self pride, to become so full of oneself to break and become a "dyspeptic old woman" (full of oneself, unable to even digest). "To be a real Philosopher is the thing, a good thing. The True Philosopher is heroic in his self-assurance and self-possession, but wonderfully un-self-conscious. The False Philosopher proclaims himself Philosopher, self-consciously and pretentiously." Scott Norsworthy

most others, they were the very magnets that thus drew me. I'll try a pagan friend, since Christian kindness has proved but hollow courtesy. I drew my bench near him and made some friendly signs and hints, doing my best to talk with him.

He seemed to take to me quite as naturally as I to him; he pressed his forehead against mine, clasped me round the waist, and said that henceforth we were married; meaning, in his country's phrase, that we were bosom friends; he would gladly die for me if the need should be. In a countryman, this sudden flame of friendship would have seemed far too premature, a thing to be much distrusted, but in this simple savage, those old rules would not apply.

After supper and another social chat and smoke, we went to our room together. He then went about his evening prayers and took out his idol. I thought he seemed anxious for me to join him and I deliberated a moment whether, in case he invited me, I would comply.

I was a good Christian, born and bred in the bosom of the infallible Presbyterian Church. How then could I unite with this wild idolator in worshiping his piece of wood? But what is worship? Do you suppose now, Ishmael, that the magnanimous God of heaven and earth—pagans and all included—can possibly be jealous of an insignificant bit of black wood? Impossible! But what is worship?—to do the will of God—*that* is worship. And what is the will of God?—to do to my fellow man what I would have my fellow man to do to me—*that* is the will of God. Now, Queequeg is my fellow man. And what do I wish that this Queequeg would do to me? Why unite with me in my particular Presbyterian form of worship. Consequently, I must then unite with him in his; I must turn idolator. So I kindled the shavings; offered the idol burnt biscuit with Queequeg; kneeled before him twice; kissed his nose; and that done, we undressed and went to bed, at peace with our own consciences and all the world. But we did not go to sleep without a little chat.

How it is, I know not; but there is no place like a bed for confidential disclosures between friends. Man and wife, they say, they open the very bottom of their souls to each other; and some old couples often lie and chat over old times till nearly morning. Thus, then, in our hearts' honeymoon, lay I and Queequeg—a cozy, loving pair.[71]

---

71   Is Ishmael gay? Was Melville gay? Though debatable, there is ample evidence to build a strong case. Some scholars have pointed to Melville's feelings towards Nathaniel Hawthorne (the author of The Scarlet Letter) as being more than platonic. Melville and Hawthorne were neighbors and spent much time together "discussing the Universe with a bottle of brandy & cigars." Moby Dick, of course, was dedicated to Hawthorne. Printed immediately after the title page the words "In Token of My Admiration for his Genius, This Book is inscribed to Nathanial [sic] Hawthorne." Nathaniel's name ironically and mysteriously misspelled.

Chapter 11. Queequeg

Queequeg was a native of Rokovoko[72], an island far away to the West and South. It is not down in any map; true places never are.[73]

Something in Queequeg's ambitious soul lurked a strong desire to see more of Christendom than a specimen whaler or two. His father was a High Chief, a King; his uncle a High Priest; and on the maternal side, he boasted aunts who were the wives of unconquerable warriors. There was excellent blood in his veins—royal stuff; though sadly spoiled, I fear, by the cannibal propensity he nourished in his untutored youth.

A Sag Harbor[74] ship visited his father's bay, and Queequeg sought a passage to Christian lands. But the ship was full; and the King his father's influence couldn't prevail. But Queequeg vowed a vow. Alone in his canoe, he paddled off to a distant strait, which he knew the ship must pass through when she left the island. Hiding his canoe, still afloat, among the thickets, he sat down in the stern, paddle low in hand; and when the ship was gliding by, like a flash he darted out; grabbed her side; with one backward dash of his foot capsized and sank his canoe; climbed up the chains, and throwing himself at full length upon the deck, grappled a ring-bolt there, and swore not to let it go, though hacked in pieces.

---

72   Melville was famously inspired to write *Moby Dick* after hearing the story of the whaler ship Essex and it's Captain Pollard. In 1820, a giant sperm whale, apparently 85 feet long (the average is 50ft) attacked and sank the whaleship. The cause of aggression is unknown. The crew were left adrift in three whaleboats (lighter boats used in the capture of whales) thousands of miles from land. Examining the charts, the officers deduced that the closest known islands, the Marqueasas, were the closest, but the crew feared they were inhabited by cannibals, so they sailed east instead for South America. Without food and water, the crew started dying and the others devolved into cannibalism. The crew drew lots to determine the next to be shot and eaten. The lot fell to Owen Coffin, the youngest of the crew, and the Captain's cousin. Bravely, he accepted his fate. Once the remaining crew arrived in Nantucket, the surviving crewmen of the *Essex* were welcomed, largely without judgment. Cannibalism in the most dire of circumstances, it was reasoned, was a custom of the sea. Captain Pollard, however, was not as easily forgiven, because he had eaten his cousin. Owen Coffin's mother could not abide being in the captain's presence. Pollard spent the rest of his life in Nantucket. Once a year, on the anniversary of the wreck of the *Essex*, he was said to have locked himself in his room and fasted in honor of his lost crewmen.

73   Literalism is the lowest form of meaning.

74   A quaint East Hampton, but very "un-hampton" village in New York. Susann Farrell, a children's librarian, said of living in Sag Harbor: "To live in a place in the 21st century where a children's librarian is a rock star in a community where rock stars actually live is truly remarkable."

In vain, the captain threatened to throw him overboard, suspended a cutlass[75] over his naked wrists; Queequeg was the son of a King, and Queequeg budged not.

Struck by his desperate dauntlessness and his wild desire to visit Christendom, the captain at last relented and told him he might make himself at home. But this fine young savage—this sea Prince of Wales, never saw the Captain's cabin. They put him down among the sailors and made a whaleman of him.

While at the bottom—so he told me—he was motivated by a profound desire to learn among the Christians how to make his people still happier than they were; and, more than that, still better than they were. But, alas! The practices of whalemen soon convinced him that even Christians could be both miserable and wicked, infinitely more so than all his father's heathens. And thus an old idolator at heart, he yet lived among these Christians, wore their clothes, and tried to talk their gibberish.

I asked him whether he would like to go back and have a coronation; since he might now consider his father dead and gone, he was very old and feeble at the last accounts. He answered no, not yet, and added that he was fearful Christianity, or rather Christians, had unfitted him for ascending the pure and undefiled throne of thirty pagan Kings before him. But, he said, he would return—as soon as he felt himself baptized again. For the time being, however, he proposed to sail about and sow his wild oats in all four oceans. They had made a harpooneer of him, and that barbed iron replaced the sceptre[76] for now.

I asked him about his plans. He answered, to go to sea again, in his old vocation. I told him that I wanted to go whaling and informed him of my intention to sail out of Nantucket. He resolved to accompany me, to which I joyously assented; for besides the affection I now felt for Queequeg, he was an experienced harpooneer, and as such, could not fail to be of great usefulness to one, who, like me, was wholly ignorant of the mysteries of whaling, though well acquainted with the sea, as known to merchant seamen.

His story ended with his pipe's last dying puff. Queequeg embraced me, pressed his forehead against mine, and blowing out the light, we rolled over from each other, this way and that, and very soon were sleeping.

---

75   A pirate short sword with a slightly curved blade

76   A staff or wand held in the hand by a ruling monarch.

Chapter 12. Nantucket

Next morning, Monday, I settled my own and comrade's bill, using, however, my comrade's money. The grinning landlord, seemed amazingly tickled at the sudden friendship which had sprung up between Queequeg and me—especially as Peter Coffin's[77] cock and bull stories about him alarmed me so.

We borrowed a wheelbarrow and gathered our things, including my own poor carpet-bag and Queequeg's canvas sack and hammock, away we went down to "the Moss," the little Nantucket packet schooner docked at the wharf. As we were going along, the people stared; not at Queequeg so much—for they were used to seeing cannibals like him in their streets—but at seeing him and me upon such friendly terms. But we paid no attention, going along wheeling the barrow by turns.

With passage paid, and luggage safe, we stood on board the schooner. Hoisting sail, it glided down the Acushnet river[78]. On one side, New Bedford rose in terraces of streets, their ice-covered trees all glittering in the clear, cold air.

For some time, we did not notice the jeering glances of the passengers, who marveled at our friendship. But there were some boobies and bumpkins there, who, by their intense greenness, must have come from the heart and center of all verdure[79]. Queequeg caught one of these young saplings mimicking him behind his back. I thought the bumpkin's hour of doom was come. Dropping his harpoon, the brawny savage caught him in his arms, and by an almost miraculous dexterity and strength, sent him high up bodily into the air; the fellow landed with bursting lungs upon his feet, while Queequeg, turning his back upon him, lighted his tomahawk pipe and passed it to me for a puff.

---

77   Owen Coffin, the unfortunate decedent of the whaling ship *Essex* was a direct lineal descendant of Tristram Coffin, one of the colonizers of Nantucket island.

78   On the Acushnet river is a Moby Dick Marina, a nice place to sit and watch boats ride by.

79   According to the Google "usage over time" chart, verdure is a word that, though popular in the early 1800's, has completely dropped from our modern vernacular. Its definition is "the greenness of growing vegetation" but used in the context of "bumpkins and intense greenness", Melville is telling us that these passengers were unsophisticates from the countryside.

"Capting! Capting!" yelled the bumpkin, running towards that officer; "Capting, Capting, here's the devil."

"Hallo, *you* sir," cried the Captain, stalking up to Queequeg, "what in thunder do you mean by that? Don't you know you might have killed that chap?"

"What him say?" said Queequeg, as he mildly turned to me.

"He say that you came near kill-e that man there," pointing to the still shivering greenhorn.

"Kill-e," cried Queequeg, twisting his tattooed face into an unearthly expression of disdain, "ah! him small-e fish-e; Queequeg no kill-e so small-e fish-e; Queequeg kill-e big whale!"

"Look you," roared the Captain, "I'll kill-e *you*, you cannibal if you try any more of your tricks aboard here, so mind your eye."

But it so happened just then that it was high time for the Captain to mind his own eye. The prodigious strain upon the main-sail had parted the weather-sheet[80], and the tremendous boom was now flying from side to side, completely sweeping the entire deck. The poor fellow whom Queequeg had handled so roughly was swept overboard; all hands were in a panic.

The boom from right to left and back again, and every instant seemed ready to snap into splinters. In the midst of this panic, Queequeg dropped deftly to his knees, and crawling under the path of the boom, whipped hold of a rope, caught it round the boom as it swept over his head, and at the next jerk, the boom was stopped, and all was safe.

Then, Queequeg stripped to the waist and darted from the side of the boat like a living arc. For three minutes or more, he was seen swimming like a dog, but saw no one to be saved. The greenhorn had gone down. Shooting himself perpendicularly from the water, Queequeg now took an instant's glance around him and, dived down and disappeared. A few minutes more, and he rose again, one arm still striking out and with the other dragging a lifeless form. The boat soon picked them up. The poor bumpkin was restored. All hands voted

---

80   In nautical usage the term "sheet" is applied to a rope or chain attached to the lower corners of a sail for the purpose of extension or change of direction.

Queequeg a hero; the captain begged his pardon. From that hour, I clove to Queequeg like a barnacle; yea, till poor Queequeg took his last[81] long dive.

He did not seem to think that he at all deserved a medal, he only asked for water—freshwater—something to wipe the brine off; and that done, he put on dry clothes, lit his pipe, and leaning against the bulwarks, and mildly eyeing those around him, seemed to be saying—"It's a mutual, joint-stock world. We cannibals must help these Christians."

Nothing more happened on the passage worthy mentioning, so, after a fine run, we safely arrived in Nantucket. Nantucket![82] Take out your map and look at it. See what a real corner of the world it occupies; how it stands offshore, more lonely than the Eddystone lighthouse.[83] Look at it—a mere mound and elbow of sand, all beach, without a background. There is more sand there than you would use in twenty years as a substitute for blotting paper[84].

The Nantucketer[85], he alone resides on the sea; in Bible language, goes down to it in ships[86]. *There* is his home; *there* lies his business. Noah's flood would not interrupt, though it overwhelmed all the millions in China. He lives on the sea and hides among the waves.

Some will tell you that they have to plant weeds there, they don't grow naturally; that they import Canada thistles; that they have to send beyond seas for a spile[87] to stop a leak in an oil cask; that pieces of wood in Nantucket are carried about like bits of the true cross in Rome[88]. But these extravaganzas only show that Nantucket is no Illinois.

What wonder, then, that these Nantucketers, born on a beach, take to the sea for a livelihood!

---

81   Foreshadow of Queequeg's final dive, after encountering Moby Dick.

82   Melville had not visited Nantucket before writing Moby Dick. His descriptions of the place came from whaler friends from Nantucket as well as his reading of "The History of Nantucket" by Obed Macy.

83   The Eddystone lighthouse has an ominous history, being four times rebuilt. The first was swept away to sea. The second burned by a fire. The third had to be dismantled because the foundation was cracking. The fourth and current edifice stands isolated, 14 miles from Plymouth.

84   A highly absorbent type of writing paper used to absorb excess ink from its surface. Blotting paper appeared in the 1840's. Prior to blotting paper, people sprinkled sand on paper to absorb ink.

85   "Nantucket seemed to offer a safe retreat from the spirit of persecution then prevailing, and persons of various denominations removed thither with their families." (The History of Nantucket 1835).

86   Psalm 107:23: "They that go down to the sea in ships, that do business in great waters."

87   Small wooden peg.

88   Highly valued and revered. Nantucket is a beach with no vegetation or trees.

Chapter 13. Clam or Cod?

It was quite late in the evening when the little Moss came snugly to anchor, and Queequeg and I went ashore; so we could attend to no business that day, at least none but a supper and a bed. The landlord of the Spouter-Inn had recommended us to his cousin Hosea[89] Hussey of the Try Pots, whom he asserted to be the proprietor of one of the best-kept hotels in all Nantucket, and moreover, he had assured us that Cousin Hosea, as he called him, was famous for his chowders.

In short, he plainly hinted that we could not possibly do better than try pot-luck at the Try Pots.

"Come on, Queequeg," I said, "all right. There's Mrs. Hussey."

Upon making known our desires for a supper and a bed, Mrs. Hussey ushered us into a little room and seating us at a table spread turned round to us and said—"Clam or Cod?"

"What's that about Cods, ma'am?" I said, with much politeness in my voice.

"Clam or Cod?" she repeated.

"A clam for supper? a cold clam; is *that* what you mean, Mrs. Hussey?" I asked, "but that's a rather cold and clammy reception in the wintertime, ain't it, Mrs. Hussey?"

But being in a great hurry to resume scolding the man in the purple[90] Shirt, who was waiting for it in the entry, and seeming to hear nothing but the word "clam," Mrs. Hussey hurried towards an open door leading to the kitchen and bawling out "clam for two," disappeared.

"Queequeg," I asked, "do you think one clam will feed us both?"

---

89   In the Bible, the Lord commands Hosea to marry a prostitute, named Gomer, a symbolic union of the relationship of Jehovah with his unfaithful people of Israel.

90   Mark 15:16-17: The soldiers led Jesus away into the palace and called together the whole company of soldiers. They put a purple robe on him, then twisted together a crown of thorns and set it on him.

When that smoking chowder came in, the mystery was delightfully explained. Oh, sweet friends! Listen to me. It was made of small juicy clams, scarcely bigger than hazel nuts, mixed with pounded ship biscuit, and salted pork cut up into little flakes; the whole enriched with butter, and plentifully seasoned with pepper and salt. Our appetites being sharpened by the frosty voyage, and in particular, Queequeg seeing his favorite fishing food before him, and the chowder being surpassingly excellent, we dispatched it with great expedition: when leaning back a moment, I thought I would try a little experiment. Stepping to the kitchen door, I uttered the word "cod" with great emphasis and took my seat. In a few moments, the savory steam came forth again, but with a different flavor, and in good time a fine cod-chowder was placed before us.

We resumed business, and while employing our spoons in the bowl, I thought to myself, I wonder if this here has any effect on the head? What's that saying about chowder-headed[91] people? "But look, Queequeg, ain't that a live eel in your bowl? Where's your harpoon?"

The Fishiest of all fishy places was the Try Pots. Chowder for breakfast, and chowder for dinner, and chowder for supper, till you began to look for fish-bones coming through your clothes. The area before the house was paved with clam-shells. Mrs. Hussey wore a polished necklace of codfish vertebra. There was a fishy flavor to the milk, too, which I could not at all account for, till one morning happening to take a stroll along the beach among some fishermen's boats, I saw Hosea's[92] cow feeding on fish remnants.

Supper concluded, we received a lamp and directions from Mrs. Hussey concerning the nearest way to bed, but, as Queequeg was about to precede me up the stairs, the lady reached forth her arm and demanded his harpoon; she allowed no harpoon in her chambers. "Why not?" I asked; "every true whaleman sleeps with his harpoon—then why not?" "Because it's dangerous," she replied. "I don't allow such dangerous weepons in rooms at night. So, Mr. Queequeg" (for she had learned his name), I will just take this here iron, and keep it for you till morning. Chowder; clam or cod to-morrow for breakfast, men?"

"Both," says I, "and let's have a couple of smoked herring by way of variety."

---

91   At the time that Melville wrote Moby Dick, the term chowder head was newly born from a British term "chowterhead", meaning stupid person. You may see Green Bay Packers fans wearing as hats, bright yellow blocks of cheese, unaware as they must be of the meaning.

92   Hosea 4:16: "For Israel is stubborn Like a stubborn calf; Now the LORD will let them forage Like a lamb in open country."

Chapter 14. Finding the Pequod

In bed, we concocted our plans for the morning. But to my surprise and no small concern, Queequeg told me that he had been diligently consulting Yojo—the name of his little black god—and Yojo earnestly urged that the selection of the ship should rest wholly with me.

I have forgotten to mention that, in many things, Queequeg placed great confidence in the excellence of Yojo's judgment and surprising forecast of things; and cherished Yojo with considerable esteem, as a rather good sort of god, who perhaps meant well enough upon the whole, but in all cases did not succeed in his benevolent designs.

Now, this plan of Queequeg's, or rather Yojo's, concerning the selection of our craft; I did not like that plan at all. I'd rather rely upon Queequeg's sagacity[93] to point out the whaler best fitted to carry us and our fortunes securely.

Next morning early, leaving Queequeg shut up with Yojo in our little bedroom—for it seemed that it was some sort of Lent or Ramadan, or day of fasting, humiliation, and prayer with Queequeg and Yojo that day—leaving Queequeg, then, fasting on his tomahawk pipe, and Yojo warming himself at his sacrificial fire of shavings, I sallied out among the shipping. After much prolonged sauntering and many random inquiries, I learned that there were three ships up for three-year voyages—The Devil-dam, the Tit-bit, and the Pequod. *Devil-Dam*, I do not know the origin of; *Tit-bit* is obvious[94]; *Pequod*, you will no doubt remember, was the name of a celebrated tribe of Massachusetts Indians; now extinct as the ancient Medes. I peered and pried about the Devil-dam; from her, hopped over to the Tit-bit; and finally, going on board the Pequod, looked around her for a moment, and then decided that this was the very ship for us.

You may have seen many a quaint craft in your day, but take my word for it, you never saw such a rare old craft as this same rare old Pequod. She was a ship of the old school. Long

---

93   Wise and insightful, sage.

94   "What is obvious is the innuendo that a devil's mother gets her teat bitten." Harrison Hayford in commentary on Moby-Dick.

seasoned, and weather-stained in the typhoons and calms of all four oceans. A noble craft, but somehow a most melancholy! All noble things are touched with that.

I looked about the deck, for some one having authority, in order to propose myself as a candidate for the voyage, at first I saw nobody; but then I saw a strange sort of tent, or rather wigwam pitched a little behind the main-mast. It seemed only a temporary erection used in port. I soon found one who seemed to have authority; and who, it being noon, and the ship's work suspended, was now enjoying a respite from the burden of command. He was seated on an old-fashioned oak chair, wriggling all over with curious movement.

There was nothing special about the appearance of the elderly man I saw; he was brown and brawny, like most old seamen, and heavily rolled up in blue pilot-cloth, cut in the Quaker[95] style.

"Is this the Captain of the Pequod?" I asked, advancing to the door of the tent.

"Supposing I was the captain of the Pequod, what would you want of me?" he demanded.

"I was thinking of shipping."

"You were, were you? I see you aren't a Nantucketer—ever been in a stove boat?"

"No, Sir, I never have."

"Do you know anything at all about whaling. I dare say—eh?

"Nothing, Sir, but I have no doubt I shall soon learn. I've been several voyages in the merchant service, and I think that—"

"Merchant service be damned. Don't speak that lingo with me. You see that leg?—I'll take that leg away from your stern if you ever talk of the merchant service to me again. Merchant

95 Melville was familiar with Quakers and their religion and they were the subject in many of his books. Quakers were given the name because they "Tremble at the Name of the Lord." There was a large population of Quakers in the whaling industry and Nantucket that became preoccupied with money, business and wealth. Ahab was a Quaker, of the whaling rebellious sort, still conditioned with religious notions of God, justice and sin.

service indeed! I suppose now ye feel considerable proud of having served in those merchant ships. Hell! man, what makes you want to go a whaling, eh?

I protested my innocence of these things. I saw that under the mask of these half humorous innuendoes, this old seaman, as an insulated Quakerish Nantucketer, was full of his insular prejudices and rather distrustful of all aliens, unless they hailed from Cape Cod or the Vineyard.

"But why a-whaling? I want to know that before I think of hiring you on board."

"Well, sir, I want to see what whaling is. I want to see the world."

"Want to see what whaling is, eh? Have you yet seen Captain Ahab?"

"Who is Captain Ahab, sir?"

"Aye, aye, I thought so. Captain Ahab is the Captain of this ship."

"I am mistaken then. I thought I was speaking to the Captain himself."

"You are speaking to Captain Peleg[96]—that's who ye are speaking to, young man. It's up to me and Captain Bildad to see the Pequod is fit for the voyage, and supplied with all her needs, including a crew. We are part owners and agents. But as I was going to say, before you decide what whaling is, you should turn your eye on Captain Ahab, young man, and you will find that he has only one leg."

"What do you mean, sir? Was the other one lost by a whale?"

"Lost by a whale! Young man, come nearer to me: it was devoured, chewed up, crunched by the monstrousest sperm whale that ever chipped a boat!—ah, ah!"

I was a little alarmed by his energy and staggered, but go a-whaling I must, and I would, and the Pequod was as good a ship as any—I thought the best—and all this I now repeated to Peleg. Seeing me so determined, he expressed his willingness to ship me.

---

96   According to the bible, it was during the time of Peleg that "the earth was divided." (Genesis 10:25).

"And thou mayest as well sign the papers right off," he added—"come along." And so he led the way below deck into the cabin.

Seated in the cabin was what seemed to me a most uncommon and surprising figure. It turned out to be Captain Bildad[97], who along with Captain Peleg was one of the largest owners of the vessel; the other shares, as is sometimes the case in these ports, being held by a crowd of old widows and fatherless children; each owning about the value of a nail or two in the ship. People in Nantucket invest their money in whaling vessels, the same way that you do yours in approved state stocks bringing in good interest.

Now, Bildad, like Peleg, and indeed many other Nantucketers, was a Quaker, the island having been originally[98] settled by that sect; to this day, its inhabitants, in general, retain in an uncommon measure the peculiarities of the Quaker. For some of these same Quakers are the most sanguinary[99] of all sailors and whale-hunters. They are fighting Quakers; they are Quakers with a vengeance.

Among them are those named with Scripture names—a common fashion on the island. Still, the audacious, daring, and boundless adventure of their lives, strangely blends with a thousand bold dashes of character, not unworthy a Scandinavian sea-king, or a poetical Pagan Roman. All men tragically great are made so through a certain morbidness. Be sure of this, O young ambition, all mortal greatness is but a disease.

Now, Bildad, I am sorry to say, had the reputation of being an incorrigible old hunks, and in his sea-going days, a bitter, hard task-master. They told me in Nantucket, though it certainly seems a curious story, that when he sailed the old Categut whaleman, his crew, upon arriving home, were mostly all carried ashore to the hospital, sore exhausted and worn out. For a pious man, especially for a Quaker, he was certainly rather hard-hearted, to say the least. He never used to swear, though, at his men, they said; but somehow, he got an inordinate quantity of cruel, unmitigated hard work out of them.

---

97   Bildad in the Bible was one of Job's three friends. At first his intent was consolation, but he became an accuser, asking Job what he had done to deserve God's wrath. (Job 2:11).

98   Nantucket was originally discovered in 1602 by a Captain Gosnold, an explorer, who was religious but was not a Quaker. He died of unknown causes at the age of 36 after a three week illness. In 1659, Thomas Macy, a Quaker protector who was once fined 30 shillings for providing shelter to Quakers during a rainstorm, purchased Nantucket from Native Americans. The island soon became a safe haven for Quakers.

99   A term that is rarely used today, but often used in the whaling industry. It means bloodthirsty.

Such, then, was the person that I saw seated on the transom when I followed Captain Peleg down into the cabin. The space between the decks was small, and there, bolt-upright, sat old Bildad, who always sat so, and never leaned, and this to save his coattails. His broad-brim hat was placed beside him; his legs were stiffly crossed, and spectacles on his nose, he seemed absorbed in reading from a ponderous volume.

"Bildad," cried Captain Peleg, "at it again, Bildad, eh? Ye have been studying those Scriptures, now, for the last thirty years, to my knowledge. How far ye got, Bildad?"

As if long used to such profane talk from his old shipmate, Bildad, without noticing his present irreverence, quietly looked up, and seeing me, glanced again inquiringly towards Peleg.

"He says he's our man, Bildad," said Peleg, "he wants to ship."

"Do you?" asked Bildad, in a hollow tone, and turning around to me.

"I *do*," I said unconsciously. He was so intense a Quaker.

"What do ye think of him, Bildad?" said Peleg.

"He'll do," said Bildad, eyeing me, and then went back at his book in a mumbling tone, though quite audibly.

I thought him the strangest old Quaker I ever saw, especially as Peleg, his friend and old shipmate, seemed such a blusterer[100]. But I said nothing, only looking around me sharply. Peleg now threw open a chest, and pulled out the ship's articles, placed pen and ink before him, and seated himself at a little table. I began to think it was high time to settle with myself at what terms I would be willing to engage for the voyage. I was already aware that in the whaling business, they paid no wages, but all hands, including the captain, received certain shares of the profits called *lays* and that these lays were proportioned to the degree of importance pertaining to the respective duties of the ship's company. I was also aware that being a green hand at whaling, my own lay would not be very large; but considering that I was used to the sea, could steer a ship, splice a rope, and all that, I made no doubt that from all I had heard I should be offered at least the 275th lay—that is, the 275th part of the

---

100 Loudmouth.

clear net proceeds of the voyage, whatever that might eventually amount to. And though the 275th lay was what they call a rather *long lay*, yet it was better than nothing; and if we had a lucky voyage, might pretty nearly pay for the clothing I would wear out on it, not to speak of my three years' beef and board, for which I would not have to pay one stiver[101].

It might be said, or at least thought that this is a poor way to accumulate a fortune—and so it is, a very poor way indeed. But I am one of those that is concerned about princely fortunes and am quite content if the world is ready to board and lodge me while I am putting up at this grim sign of the Thunder Cloud[102]. Upon the whole, I thought that the 275th lay would be about the fair thing but would not have been surprised had I been offered the 200th, considering I was of a broad-shouldered build.

One thing, nevertheless, that made me a little nervous about receiving a generous share of the profits was Bildad, who never heeded us but went on mumbling to himself out of his book, "*Lay* not up for yourselves treasures upon earth, where moth—"

"Well, Captain Bildad," interrupted Peleg, "what d'ye say, what lay shall we give this young man?"

"You know best," was the reply, "the seven hundred and seventy-seventh[103] wouldn't be too much, would it?—'where moth and rust do corrupt, but *lay*—'"

Lay, indeed, I thought, and such a lay! the seven hundred and seventy-seventh! Well, old Bildad, you are determined that I, for one, shall not *lay* up many *lays* here below, where moth and rust do corrupt.

"Why, blast your eyes, Bildad," cried Peleg, "You don't want to swindle this young man! he must have more than that."

"Seven hundred and seventy-seventh," again said Bildad, without lifting his eyes, and then went on mumbling—"for where your treasure is, there will your heart be also."

---

101 A small coin used in the Netherlands in the early 1800's.

102 Pandora opens the box of sickness, death, mortality and a thundercloud falls on Epimetheus, the God of afterthought and excuses.

103 According to the Oxford study bible, the number 777 represents the threefold, perfected Trinity and can be contrasted against the number 666, representing the number of the Devil.

"I am going to put him down for the three hundredths," said Peleg, "do ye hear that, Bildad! The three hundredth[104] lay, I say."

Bildad laid down his book, and turning solemnly towards him, said, "Captain Peleg, you have a generous heart; but you must consider the duty owed to the other owners of this ship—widows and orphans, many of them—and that if we too abundantly reward the labors of this young man, we may be taking the bread from those widows and those orphans. The seven hundred and seventy-seventh lay, Captain Peleg."

"Damn you Bildad!" roared Peleg, starting up and clattering about the cabin. "Blast ye, Captain Bildad,: "Fiery pit! Fiery pit! You insult me, man; past all natural bearing, you insult me. Out of the cabin, ye canting, drab-colored son of a wooden gun!"

As he thundered out this, he made a rush at Bildad, but with a marvelous move, Bildad for that time eluded him.

Alarmed at this terrible outburst between the two principal and responsible owners of the ship, and feeling half a mind to give up all idea of sailing in a vessel so questionably owned and temporarily commanded, I stepped aside from the door to give way to Bildad, who, I made no doubt, was eager to vanish from the wrath of Peleg. But to my astonishment, he sat down again on the transom very quietly and seemed to have not the slightest intention of withdrawing. He seemed quite used to Peleg and his ways. As for Peleg, after letting off his rage as he had, there seemed no more left in him, and he, too, sat down like a lamb, though he twitched a little as if still nervously agitated. "Whew!" he whistled at last—"Now then, my young man, Ishmael's your name, didn't you say? Well then, down you go here, Ishmael, for the three hundredth lay."

"Captain Peleg," said I, "I have a friend with me who wants to ship too—shall I bring him down tomorrow?"

"Yes, sure," said Peleg. "Bring him down, and we'll look at him."

"What lay does he want?" groaned Bildad, glancing up from the book in which he had again been burying himself.

---

104 Jacob, the one sold into slavery by his brothers in Genesis, becomes the second most powerful ruler in Egypt. After an emotional revealing of his true identity to his brothers, he gifts his youngest brother Benjamin 300 pieces of silver. Genesis 45:22

"Oh! never you mind about that, Bildad," said Peleg. "Has he ever whaled it any?" turning to me.

"Killed more whales than I can count, Captain Peleg."

"Well, bring him along then."

And, after signing the papers, off, I went; nothing doubting but that I had done a good morning's work and that the Pequod was the identical ship that Yojo had provided to carry Queequeg and me round the Cape.

But I had not gone far when I began to think that the Captain with whom I was to sail yet remained unseen by me, and I should at least have a look at him before committing myself into his hands. Turning back, I asked Captain Peleg where Captain Ahab could be found.

"And what do you want of Captain Ahab?"

"I would just like to see him."

"I don't think you will be able to. I don't know exactly what's the matter with him, but he keeps close inside the house; a sort of sick, and yet he doesn't look so. In fact, he ain't sick; but no, he isn't well either. Anyhow, young man, he won't always see me, so I don't suppose he will see you. He's a strange man, Captain Ahab—so some think—but a good one. Oh, you'll like him well enough; no fear, no fear. He's a grand, ungodly, god-like man, Captain Ahab; doesn't speak much; but, when he does speak, then you may well listen. Be forewarned; Ahab's above the common; Ahab's been in colleges, as well as among the cannibals. His lance! Aye, the keenest and the surest that out of all our isle! Oh! he ain't Captain Bildad; no, and he ain't Captain Peleg; *he's Ahab*, boy; and Ahab of old, you know, was a crowned king!"

"And a very vile one. When that wicked king was slain, the dogs, did they not lick his blood?"[105]

---

105 In the Bible, Ahab is the 7th king of Israel, who did "more to provoke the anger of the Lord than any king before him." During a battle at the Jordan River, Ahab was killed by an arrow and some dogs licked his blood, as prophesied would happen by Elijah, for forsaking God's commandments.

"Come here—here, here," said Peleg, with a significance in his eye that almost startled me. "Look here, lad; never say that on board the Pequod. Never say it anywhere. Captain Ahab did not name himself."

'Twas a foolish, ignorant whim of his crazy, widowed mother, who died when he was only a year old. And yet, the old squaw said that the name would somehow prove prophetic. And, perhaps, other fools like her may tell you the same. I wish to warn you. It's a lie. I know Captain Ahab well; I've sailed with him as mate years ago; I know what he is—a good man—not a pious, good man, like Bildad, but a swearing good man—something like me—only there's a good deal more of him. Yes, I know that he was never very jolly, and I know that on the passage home, he was a little out of his mind for a spell; but it was the sharp shooting pains in his bleeding stump that brought that about, as anyone might see. I know, too, that ever since he lost his leg last voyage by that accursed whale, he's been a kind of moody—desperate moody, and savage sometimes, but that will all pass off. And once and for all, let me tell you and assure you, young man, it's better to sail with a moody good captain than a laughing bad one. So good-bye to you—and curse not Captain Ahab, because he happens to have a wicked name. Besides, my boy, he has a wife[106]—a sweet, resigned girl. Think of that; by that sweet girl that old man has a child: ask yourself then can there be any harm in Ahab? No, no, my lad; stricken, blasted maybe, but, Ahab has his humanities!"

As I walked away, I was full of thought; what had been incidentally revealed to me of Captain Ahab filled me with a certain wild vagueness of painfulness concerning him. And somehow, at the time, I felt a sympathy and a sorrow for him, but for I don't know what, unless it was the cruel loss of his leg. And yet I also felt a strange awe in him; but that sort of awe, which I cannot at all describe, was not exactly awe; I do not know what it was. But I felt it, and it did not distance me from him, though I felt what seemed like mystery in him, so imperfectly as he was known to me then. However, my thoughts were at length carried in other directions so that for the present dark Ahab slipped my mind.

---

106 The biblical Ahab married Jezebel, who was a dominant influence on Ahab, persuading him to abandon The God of Israel and establish the religion of Baal (idol worship).

Chapter 15. Ramadan

As Queequeg's Ramadan, or Fasting, was to continue all day, I did not choose to disturb him till towards night-fall; for I cherish the greatest respect towards everybody's religious obligations, never mind how comical, and could not find it in my heart to undervalue even a congregation of ants worshiping a toad-stool.

We good Presbyterian Christians should be charitable in these things and not consider ourselves so vastly superior to other mortals, pagans, and whatnot, because of their half-crazy ideas on these subjects. There was Queequeg, now, certainly entertaining the most absurd notions about Yojo and his Ramadan;—but who cares? Queequeg thought he knew what he was about, I suppose; he seemed to be content; there let him rest. All our arguing with him would not avail; let him be, I say: and Heaven have mercy on us all—Presbyterians and Pagans alike—for we are all somehow dreadfully cracked about the head, and sadly need mending.

Towards evening, when I felt assured that all his performances and rituals must be over, I went up to his room and knocked at the door; but no answer. I tried to open it, but it was fastened inside. "Queequeg," said I softly through the key-hole:—all silent. "Queequeg! Why don't you speak? It's I—Ishmael." But all remained still as before.

I began to grow alarmed. I had allowed him such abundant time; I thought he might have had an apoplectic fit[107]. I looked through the key-hole, but the door opening into an odd corner of the room, the key-hole prospect was but a crooked and sinister one.

Have to burst it open," I said, and was running down the entry a little, for a good start, when the landlady caught at me, again vowing I should not break down her premises, but I tore from her, and with a sudden bodily rush dashed myself fully against the mark.

With a loud noise, the door flew open, and the knob slammed against the wall and sent the plaster to the ceiling; and there, good heavens! There sat Queequeg, altogether cool and self-collected, right in the middle of the room, squatting on his hams and holding Yojo on

---

107 Stroke.

top of his head. He looked neither one way nor the other but sat like a carved image with scarcely a sign of active life.

"Queequeg," I asked, going up to him, "Queequeg, what's the matter with you?"

We couldn't drag a word out of him; I almost felt like pushing him over, to change his position, for it was almost intolerable, it seemed so painfully and unnaturally constrained; especially, as he had been sitting so for eight or ten hours, without his regular meals.

"Mrs. Hussey," said I, "he's *alive*, so leave us, and I will see to this strange affair myself."

Closing the door upon the landlady, I tried to get Queequeg to take a chair; but in vain. There he sat; he would not move a peg, or say a single word, or even look at me, or recognize my presence in the slightest way.

I wonder, I thought, if this can possibly be a part of his Ramadan; do they fast on their hams that way in his native island. It must be so; yes, it's part of his creed, I suppose; well, then, let him rest; he'll get up sooner or later, no doubt. It can't last forever, thank God, and his Ramadan only comes once a year; and I don't believe it's very punctual then.

I went down to supper. After sitting a long time listening to the long stories of some sailors who had just come from a voyage, I went upstairs to go to bed, feeling quite sure by this time Queequeg must certainly have brought his Ramadan to an end. But no; there he was just where I had left him; he had not stirred an inch. It seemed so downright senseless and insane to be sitting there all day and half the night on his hams in a cold room, holding a piece of wood on his head.

"For heaven's sake, Queequeg, get up and shake yourself; get up and have some supper. You'll starve; you'll kill yourself, Queequeg." But he did not reply; not a word.

I determined to go to bed and to sleep, and no doubt, before a great while, he would follow me. It took some time, but somehow I fell asleep at last and didn't wake until morning; when looking over the bedside, there squatted Queequeg, as if he had been screwed down to the floor. But as soon as the first glimpse of sun entered the window, he got up, with stiff and grating joints, but with a cheerful look; limped towards me where I lay; pressed his forehead again against mine; and said his Ramadan was over.

Now, as I before expressed, I have no objection to any person's religion, be it what it may, so long as that person does not kill or insult any other person because that other person doesn't believe it also. But when a man's religion becomes really frantic; when it is a positive torment to him; and, in fine, makes this earth of ours an uncomfortable inn to lodge in; then I think it high time to take that individual aside and argue the point with him.

And just so I now did with Queequeg. "Queequeg," I said, "get into bed now, and listen to me." I then went on, beginning with the rise and progress of the primitive religions and coming down to the various religions of the present time, during which time I labored to show Queequeg that all these Lents, Ramadans, and prolonged ham-squattings in the cold, cheerless rooms were stark nonsense; bad for the health; useless for the soul; opposed, in short, to the obvious laws of Hygiene and common sense.

I told him, too, that as he was such an extremely sensible and clever savage, it pained me, very badly pained me, to see him now so deplorably foolish about this ridiculous Ramadan of his. Besides, I argued, fasting makes the body cave in; hence the spirit caves in, and all thoughts born of a fast must necessarily be half-starved. This is the reason why most dyspeptic[108] religionists cherish are so melancholy. In a word, Queequeg, I said, rather digressively; hell is an idea first born on an undigested apple-dumpling[109] and since then perpetuated through hereditary indigestion nurtured by Ramadans.

I do not think that my remarks about religion made much impression upon Queequeg. Because, in the first place, he somehow seemed dull of hearing on that important subject, unless considered from his own point of view; and, in the second place, he did not more than one third understand me, and, finally, he no doubt thought he knew a good deal more about the true religion than I did. He looked at me with a sort of condescending concern and compassion, as though he thought it a great pity that such a sensible young man should be so hopelessly lost to evangelical pagan piety.

At last, we rose and dressed; and Queequeg, taking a hearty breakfast of chowders of all sorts, so that the landlady should not make much profit by reason of his Ramadan, we sallied out to board the Pequod, sauntering along, and picking our teeth with halibut bones.

---

108 Indigestion or consequent irritability or depression.

109 Apple dumplings came to American by way of the Pennsylvania Dutch. Known as a "poor man's alternative to meat", it was a cheaper way to satisfy hunger.

Chapter 16. The Mark

As we were walking down the end of the wharf towards the ship, Queequeg carrying his harpoon, Captain Peleg in his gruff voice loudly hailed us from his wigwam, saying he had not suspected my friend was a cannibal, and that he doesn't let cannibals on board that craft, unless they properly produce their papers.

"What do you mean by that, Captain Peleg?" I asked, now jumping on the bulwarks and leaving my comrade standing on the wharf.

"I mean," he replied, "he must show his papers."

"Yes," said Captain Bildad in his hollow voice, sticking his head from behind Peleg's out of the wigwam. "He must show that he's converted. Son of darkness[110]," he added, turning to Queequeg, "art thou at present in communion with any Christian church?"

"Why," I said, "he's a member of the First Congregational Church." Here be it said that many tattooed savages sailing in Nantucket ships, at last, come to be converted into the churches.

"First Congregational Church," cried Bildad, "what! They worship in Deacon Deuteronomy Coleman's meeting-house?" and taking out his spectacles, he rubbed them with his great yellow bandana handkerchief, and putting them on very carefully, came out of the wigwam, and leaning stiffly over the bulwarks[111], took a good long look at Queequeg.

"How long has he been a member?" he asked, turning to me. "And he hasn't been baptized right either, or it would have washed some of that devil's blue off his face."

"So tell me," cried Bildad, "is this Philistine[112] a regular member of Deacon Deuteronomy's meeting? I've never seen him going there, and I pass it every Lord's day."

---

110 A fragment of the dead sea scrolls called the war scroll lays an apocalyptic framework where the sons of light will be pitted against the sons of darkness in a final battle royale.

111 An extension of a ship's sides above the level of the deck.

112 In the 19th century, this derogatory term was used to describe "an enemy to God." Well known is the story of the great Goliath, a Philistine, killed by David of the clan Judah.

"I don't know anything about Deacon Deuteronomy or his meeting," I said; "all I know is that Queequeg here is a born member of the First Congregational Church. He is a deacon himself, Queequeg is."

Without saying a word, Queequeg, in his wild sort of way, jumped upon the bulwarks, from thence into the bows of one of the whale-boats hanging to the side; and then bracing his left knee, and poising his harpoon, cried out:—

"Captain, you see him small drop tar on water dere? Do you see him? Well, spose him one whale eye, well, den!" and taking sharp aim at it, he darted the iron right over old Bildad's broad brim, clean across the ship's decks, and struck the glistening tar spot out of sight.

"Now," said Queequeg, quietly hauling in the line, "spos-ee him whale-e eye; why, dad whale dead."

"Quick, Bildad," said Peleg, his partner, who, aghast at the close vicinity of the flying harpoon, had retreated towards the cabin. "Quick, I say, Bildad, and get the ship's papers. We must have Hedgehog[113] there, I mean Quohog, in one of our boats. Look ye, Quohog, we'll give ye the ninetieth lay, and that's more than ever was given a harpooneer yet out of Nantucket."

So down we went into the cabin, and to my great joy, Queequeg was soon enrolled among the same ship's company to which I myself belonged.

---

113 The term hedgehog was synonymous with street urchin, which according to the urban dictionary of the time meant a "grubby looking child who roamed the streets".

Chapter 17. The Prophet

Shipmates, have ye shipped in that ship?"

Queequeg and I had just left the Pequod and were sauntering away from the water, for the moment each occupied with his own thoughts when the above words were put to us by a shabbily apparelled stranger, who, pausing before us, leveled his massive forefinger at the vessel in question.

"Have ye shipped in her?" he repeated.

"You mean the ship Pequod, I suppose," I said, trying to gain a little more time for an uninterrupted look at him.

"Aye, the Pequod—that ship there," he said, drawing back his whole arm and then rapidly shoving it straight out from him, with the fixed bayonet of his pointed finger darted full at the object.

"Yes, we have just signed the articles."

"Anything down there about your souls?" This strange man inquired.

"About what?"

"Oh, perhaps you hav'n't got any," he said quickly.

"Queequeg," said I, "let's go; this fellow has broken loose from somewhere; he's talking about something and somebody we don't know."

"Stop!" cried the stranger. "Ye said true—ye hav'n't seen Old Thunder yet, have ye?"

"Who's Old Thunder?" said I, again riveted with the insane earnestness of his manner.

"Captain Ahab."

What! the captain of our ship, the Pequod?"

"Aye, among some of us old sailor chaps, he goes by that name. Ye hav'n't seen him yet, have ye?"

"No, we hav'n't. He's sick they say, but is getting better and will be all right again before long."

"All right again before long!" laughed the stranger, with a solemnly derisive sort of laugh.

"What do you know about him?"

"What did they *tell* you about him?"

"They didn't tell much of anything about him; I've heard that he's a good whale-hunter and a good captain to his crew."

"That's true, that's true—yes, both true enough. But you must jump when he gives an order. Step and growl; growl and go—that's the word with Captain Ahab. But nothing about that thing that happened to him off Cape Horn, long ago, when he lay like dead for three days and nights[114]; heard nothing about that, eh? And nothing about his losing his leg last voyage, according to the prophecy?

"Ye've shipped, have ye? Names down on the papers? Well, well, what's signed, is signed; and what's to be, will be; and then again, perhaps it won't be, after all."

"Come along, Queequeg, let's leave this crazy man. But stop, tell me your name, will you?"

"Elijah[115]."

Elijah! I thought, and we walked away, both commenting upon this ragged old sailor, and agreed that he was nothing but a humbug.

---

114 Matthew 12: 40: For as Jonas was three days and three nights in the whale's belly; so shall the Son of man be three days and three nights in the heart of the earth.

115 In the bible, Elijah was a prophet who told King Ahab to repent or he would be killed and the dogs would lick up his blood. 1 Kings 21:19.

Chapter 18. All Astir

A day or two passed, and there was great activity aboard the Pequod. During these days of preparation, Queequeg and I often visited the craft, and I asked about Captain Ahab, and how he was, and when he was going to come on board his ship. To these questions, they would answer that he was getting better and better and was expected aboard every day; meantime, the two captains, Peleg and Bildad, could attend to everything necessary to fit the vessel for the voyage.

If I had been downright honest with myself, I would have seen very plainly in my heart that I did not like being committed to such a long voyage without once laying my eyes on the man who was to be the absolute dictator of it. But when a man suspects any wrong, it sometimes happens that if he is already involved in the matter, he insensibly strives to cover up his suspicions even from himself. And much this way, it was with me. I said nothing and tried to think nothing.

At last we were told that sometime the next day, the ship would sail. So the next morning, Queequeg and I took a very early start.

It was nearly six o'clock, a grey imperfect misty dawn when we drew nigh to the wharf.

"Hey there!" cried a voice. It was Elijah.

"Going aboard?"

"Go away, will you," I said.

"Lookee here," said Queequeg, "go away!"

"Ain't going aboard, then?"

"Yes, we are," I said, "but what business is that of yours? Do you know, Mr. Elijah, that I consider you a little impertinent?"

"No, no, no; I wasn't aware of that," said Elijah, slowly and wonderingly looking from me to Queequeg.

"Elijah," I said, "you will please leav us alone. We are going to the Indian and Pacific Oceans and would prefer not to be detained."

"Oh! I was going to warn you against—but never mind, never mind—it's all one, all in the family too;—sharp frost this morning, ain't it? Good-bye to ye. Shan't see ye again very soon, I guess; unless it's before the Grand Jury[116]."

And with these cracked words, he finally departed, leaving me, for the moment, in no small wonderment at his frantic impertinence.

At last, stepping on board the Pequod, we found everything in profound quiet, not a soul moving.

---

116 Matthew 25: 31-35: When the Son of Man comes in his glory, and all the angels with him, then he will sit on the throne of his glory. All the nations will be gathered before him, and he will separate people one from another as a shepherd separates the sheep from the goats, and he will put the sheep at his right hand and the goats at the left. Then the king will say to those at his right hand, 'Come, you that are blessed by my Father, inherit the kingdom prepared for you from the foundation of the world; for I was hungry and you gave me food, I was thirsty and you gave me something to drink, I was a stranger and you welcomed me."

Chapter 19. Merry Christmas

At last, the anchor was up, the sails were set, and off we glided. It was a short, cold Christmas, and as the short northern day merged into night, we found ourselves upon the wintry ocean, whose freezing spray cased us in ice.

Lank Bildad, as the pilot, headed the first watch, and as the old craft deep dived into the green seas and sent the shivering frost all over her, and the winds howled, his steady notes were heard—

"Sweet fields beyond the swelling flood,
Stand dressed in living green.
So to the Jews old Canaan stood,
While Jordan rolled between."

Never did those sweet words sound more sweetly to me than then. They were full of hope and fruition. As for Captain Ahab, no sign of him was yet to be seen; they said he was in the cabin. But then, the idea was that his presence was by no means necessary in getting the ship underway and steering her well out to sea. Indeed, as that was not at all his proper business, but the pilot's.

Chapter 20. Bulkington

Some chapters back, one Bulkington[117] was spoken of, a tall, newlanded mariner, encountered in New Bedford at the inn.

When on that shivering winter's night, the Pequod thrust her vindictive bows into the malicious cold waves, who should I see standing at her helm but Bulkington! I looked with sympathetic awe and fearfulness upon the man, who in mid-winter just landed from a four years' dangerous voyage, could without rest push off again for still another tempestuous term. The land seemed scorching to his feet. Wonderful things are ever unmentionable; deep memories yield no epitaphs; this six-inch chapter is the stoneless grave of Bulkington.

Know ye now, Bulkington? Do you see that mortally intolerable truth; that all deep, earnest thinking is but the effort of the soul to keep the open independence of her sea. Take heart, take heart, O Bulkington! Bear thee grimly, demigod! Up from the spray of thy ocean-perishing—straight up, leaps thy apotheosis[118]!

---

117 Bulkington is a beloved character and was easy to keep even in this abridged version. Some critics have called his presence an "unnecessary duplicate" a reluctant afterthought and page filler. Others, like myself, view Bulkington as the great mythical Hercules, an inspiration of adventure, choosing "sea over port, hardship over comfort, solitude over society and intellectual freedom over dogma."

118 The elevation of someone to divine status.

Chapter 21. Starbuck[119]

The chief mate of the Pequod was Starbuck, a native of Nantucket and a Quaker by descent. He was a long, earnest man, and though born on an icy coast, seemed well adapted to endure hot latitudes, his flesh being hard as a twice-baked biscuit. Yet, for all his hardy sobriety and fortitude, he was uncommonly conscientious for a seaman and endued with deep natural reverence, the wild watery loneliness of his life did therefore strongly incline him to superstition; but to that sort of superstition which seems, somehow, from intelligence than from ignorance.

"I will have no man in my boat," said Starbuck, "who is not afraid of a whale." By this, he seemed to mean that an utterly fearless man is a far more dangerous comrade than a coward.

"Aye, aye," said Stubb, the second mate, "Starbuck, there, is as careful a man as you'll find anywhere in this fishery."

Starbuck was no crusader after perils; in him, courage was not a sentiment; but a thing simply useful to him.

Stubb was the second mate. He was a native of Cape Cod; a happy-go-lucky; neither cowardly nor valiant; taking perils as they came with an indifferent air. What, perhaps, with other things, made Stubb such an easy-going, unfearing man and helped to bring about that good-humor of his; that thing must have been his pipe. For, like his nose, his short, black little pipe was one of the regular features of his face. You would almost as soon have expected him to turn out of his bunk without his nose as without his pipe.

He kept a whole row of pipes there ready loaded, stuck in a rack, within easy reach of his hand; and, whenever he turned in, he smoked them all out in succession, lighting one from the other to the end of the chapter; then loading them again to be in readiness anew. For, when Stubb dressed, instead of first putting his legs into his trousers, he put his pipe into his mouth.

---

119 A name chosen by the popular coffee company, maybe ironically, as Starbuck proves to be the gentle, calming influence to the excitable Ahab.

The third mate was Flask, a native of Tisbury, in Martha's Vineyard. A short, stout, ruddy young fellow, very pugnacious concerning whales, who somehow seemed to think that the great leviathans had personally and hereditarily affronted him; and therefore, it was a sort of a point of honor with him, to destroy them whenever encountered. So utterly lost was he to all sense of reverence for the many marvels of their majestic bulk and mystique, and so dead to anything like an apprehension of any possible danger from encountering them; that in his poor opinion, the wondrous whale was but a species of magnified mouse, or at least water-rat. He followed these fish for the fun of it, and a three years' voyage round Cape Horn was only a jolly joke that lasted that length of time.

Now these three mates—Starbuck, Stubb, and Flask, were monumentous men. In Captain Ahab's grand battle, these three headsmen were as captains of companies.

And in this famous fishery, each mate or headsman is always accompanied by his harpooneer.

First of all was Queequeg, whom Starbuck, the chief mate, had selected for his squire. But Queequeg is already known.

Next was Tashtego, an unmixed Indian from Gay Head. To look at the tawny brawn of his snaky limbs, you would almost have credited the superstitions of some of the earlier Puritans and half-believed this wild Indian to be a son of the Prince of the Powers of the Air.[120] Tashtego was Stubb's, the second mate's squire.

Third among the harpooneers was Daggoo, a gigantic, coal-black savage with a lion-like power—an Ahasuerus[121] to behold. Suspended from his ears were two golden hoops, so large that the sailors called them ring-bolts and would talk of securing the top-sail ropes to them. In his youth, Daggoo had voluntarily shipped on board a whaler, lying in a lonely bay on his native coast. And never having been anywhere in the world but in Africa, Nantucket, and the pagan harbors most frequented by whalemen; and having now led for many years the bold life of the fishery in the ships of owners uncommonly heedful of what manner of men they shipped; Daggoo retained all his barbaric virtues, and erect as a giraffe, moved about the decks in all the pomp of six feet five in his socks. There was a corporeal humility in looking up at him, and the man standing before him seemed a white flag come to beg truce of a fortress.

---

120 Ephesians 2:2: Wherein in time past ye walked according to the course of this world, according to the prince of the power of the air, the spirit that now worketh in the children of disobedience.

121 A King in the Book of Esther, Ahasuerus was a ruler over many provinces and mighty warrior.

Chapter 22. Ahab.

For several days after leaving Nantucket, nothing was seen of Captain Ahab. Yes, their supreme lord and dictator was there, though he remained unseen by any eyes not permitted to penetrate into the now sacred retreat of the cabin.

It was one of these still grey and gloomy enough mornings of the transition when with a fair wind the ship was rushing through the water with a vindictive sort of leaping and melancholy rapidity, that as I went to the deck for the afternoon watch, shivers ran over me. Reality outran apprehension; Captain Ahab stood upon his quarter-deck.

There seemed no sign of common bodily illness about him, nor of the recovery from any. His whole high, broad form seemed made of solid bronze and shaped in an unalterable mold, like Cellini's cast Perseus[122].

So powerfully did the whole grim aspect of Ahab affect me that for the first few moments, I hardly noticed the barbaric white leg upon which he partly stood. This ivory leg had at sea been fashioned from the polished bone of the sperm whale's jaw.

I was struck with the singular posture he maintained. Captain Ahab stood erect, looking straight out beyond the ship's ever-pitching bow. There was an infinity of firmest fortitude, a determinate, non-surrenderable willfulness, in the fixed and fearless, forward dedication of that glance.

Not a word he spoke, nor did his officers say anything to him, though by all their minutest gestures and expressions, they plainly showed the uneasy, if not painful, the consciousness of being under a troubled master-eye[123]. Moody-stricken Ahab stood before them with a crucifixion in his face.

---

122 Perseus is a bronze sculpture with sword in right hand and the head of Madusa being held up by the scalp in his left hand. Made by Benvenuto Cellini in the mid 1500's, it was the first statue created of bronze in nearly half a century. The work invokes an archetype of Christ in the method in which it was created, by remelting the bronze and blowing life into the sculpture.

123 Psalms 33:18: "Behold, the eye of the Lord is on those who fear him, on those who hope in his steadfast love."

Not long, from his first visit in the air, he withdrew into his cabin. But after that morning, he was every day visible to the crew, either standing in his pivot-hole[124] or seated upon an ivory stool he had; or heavily walking the deck. As the sky grew less gloomy; indeed, he began to grow a little genial, becoming less and less a recluse; as if, when the ship had sailed from home, nothing but the dead wintry bleakness of the sea had then kept him so secluded. And soon enough he was almost continually in the air.

Nevertheless, the warm, warbling persuasiveness of the pleasant holiday weather we came to seemed gradually to charm him from his mood. More than once he put forth the faint blossom of a look, which, in any other man, would have soon flowered out in a smile.

Some days elapsed, and ice and icebergs all astern, the Pequod now went rolling through the bright Quito[125] spring. Ahab, seemed so much to live in the open air.

He stood for a while leaning over the bulwarks, and then, as had been usual with him of late, calling a sailor of the watch, he sent him below for his ivory stool and also his pipe. Lighting the pipe and planting the stool on the weather side of the deck, he sat and smoked.

Some moments passed, during which the thick vapor came from his mouth in quick and constant puffs, which blew back again into his face. "How now," he soliloquized. At last, withdrawing the tube, "this smoking no longer soothes. Oh, my pipe! How is it that your charm is gone!"

What business have I with this pipe? This thing that is meant for sereneness, to send up mild white vapors among mild white hairs, not among torn iron-grey locks like mine. I'll smoke no more—"

He tossed the still lighted pipe into the sea, and the fire hissed in the waves. With slouched hat, Ahab anxiously paced the planks.

It drew near the close of day. Suddenly he came to a halt by the bulwarks and inserting his bone leg into the auger-hole there. He ordered Starbuck to send everybody up[126].

---

124 The pivot hole is an indentation in the deck of the pequod where Ahab stands frequently with his ivory leg boring down. It balances him and allows him to circle around 360 degrees.

125 Capital of Ecuador.

126 Near.

"Sir!" said the mate, astonished at an order seldom or never given on board except in some extraordinary case.

"Send everybody up," repeated Ahab.

When the entire ship's company was assembled, and with curious and not wholly unapprehensive faces, were eyeing him, Ahab, darting his eyes among the crew, started from his standpoint; and as though not a soul was near him resumed his heavy turns upon the deck. With bent head and half-slouched hat hee continued to pace, unmindful of the wondering whispering among the men, till Stubb cautiously whispered to Flask, that Ahab must have summoned them there for the purpose of witnessing a pedestrian feat. But this did not last long. Vehemently pausing, he cried:—

"What do ye do when ye see a whale, men?"

"Sing out for him!" was the impulsive rejoinder from a score of clubbed voices.

"Good!" cried Ahab, with a wild approval in his tones.

"And what do ye next, men?"

"Lower away, and after him!"

"And what tune is it ye pull to, men?"

"A dead whale or a stove boat!"

More and more strangely and fiercely glad and approving grew the countenance of the old man at every shout while the mariners began to gaze curiously at each other as if marveling how it was that they themselves became so excited at such seemingly purposeless questions.

But, they were all eagerness again, as Ahab, now half-revolving in his pivot-hole, with one hand reaching high up a shroud[127], and tightly, almost convulsively grasping it, addressed them:—

---

127 A set of ropes forming part of the standing rigging of a sailing vessel and supporting the mast from the sides; also a cloth used for mummification or burial.

"Look ye! do'ye see this Spanish ounce of gold?"—holding up a broad bright coin to the sun—"it is a sixteen dollar piece, men. Do'ye see it? Mr. Starbuck, hand me the hammer."

While the mate was getting the hammer, Ahab, without speaking, was slowly rubbing the gold piece against the skirts of his jacket, as if to heighten its luster, and without using any words was meanwhile lowly humming to himself.

Receiving the hammer from Starbuck, he advanced towards the main-mast with the hammer uplifted in one hand, showing the gold with the other, and with a high raised voice exclaimed: "Whosoever of ye raises me a white-headed whale with a wrinkled brow and a crooked jaw; whosoever of ye raises me that white-headed whale, with three holes punctured in his starboard fluke—look ye, whosoever of ye raises me that same white whale, he shall have this gold ounce, my boys!"

"Huzza! Huzza!"[128] cried the seamen as they hailed the act of nailing the gold to the mast.

"It's a white whale, I say," resumed Ahab, "a white whale. Skin your eyes for him, men; look sharp for white water; if ye see but a bubble, sing out."

All this while Tashtego, Daggoo, and Queequeg had looked on with even more intense interest and surprise than the rest, and at the mention of the wrinkled brow and crooked jaw, they had started as if each was separately touched by some specific recollection.

"Captain Ahab," said Tashtego, "that white whale must be the same that some call Moby Dick."

"Moby Dick?" shouted Ahab. "Do ye know the white whale then, Tash?"

"Does he fan-tail a little curious, sir, before he goes down?" said the Gay-Header deliberately.

"And has he a curious spout, too," said Daggoo, "very bushy, even for a Sperm Whale, and mighty quick, Captain Ahab?"

"And he has one, two, three—oh! good many irons in him hide, too, Captain," cried Queequeg disjointedly, "all twiske-tee be-twisk, like him—him—" faltering hard for a word, and screwing his hand round and round as though uncorking a bottle—"like him—him—"

---

128 A Shakespearan term for Hip Hip Hooray!

"Corkscrew!" cried Ahab, "aye, Queequeg, the harpoons lie all twisted and wrenched in him; aye, Daggoo, his spout is a big one, like a whole shock of wheat, and white as a pile of our Nantucket wool after the great annual sheep-shearing; aye, Tashtego, and he fan-tails like a split jib in a squall. Death and devils! men, it is Moby Dick ye have seen—Moby Dick—Moby Dick!"

"Captain Ahab," said Starbuck, who, with Stubb and Flask, had thus far been eyeing his superior with increasing surprise but at last seemed struck with a thought which somewhat explained all the wonder. "Captain Ahab, I have heard of Moby Dick—but wasn't it Moby Dick that took off your leg?"

"Who told you that?" cried Ahab; then pausing, "Aye, Starbuck; aye, my hearties all round; it was Moby Dick that dismasted me; Moby Dick that brought me to this dead stump I stand on now. Aye, aye," he shouted with a terrific, loud, animal sob, like that of a heart-stricken moose; "Aye, aye! It was that accursed white whale that razed me; made a poor pegging lubber of me forever and a day!" Then tossing both arms, he shouted out: "Aye, aye! and I'll chase him round Good Hope, and round the Horn, and round the Norway Maelstrom[129], and round perdition's flames before I give him up. And this is what ye have shipped for, men! to chase that white whale on both sides of land, and over all sides of the earth, till he spouts black blood and rolls fin out. What say ye, men, will ye splice hands on it, now? I think ye do look brave."

"Aye, aye!" shouted the harpooneers and seamen, running closer to the excited old man: "A sharp eye for the white whale; a sharp lance for Moby Dick!"

"God bless ye," he seemed to half sob and half shout. "God bless ye, men! But what's this long face about, Mr. Starbuck; wilt thou not chase the white whale? are you not game for Moby Dick?"

"I am game for his crooked jaw and for the jaws of Death too, Captain Ahab if it fairly comes in the way of the business we follow, but I came here to hunt whales, not my commander's vengeance. How many barrels will your vengeance yield, Captain Ahab? it will not fetch you much in our Nantucket market."

---

129 A system of the strongest whirlpools and tidal eddies that forms in the Norwegian sea.

"Nantucket market! Hoot! But come closer, Starbuck. If money's to be the measure, man, and the accountants have computed their great counting-house the globe by girdling it with guineas, one to every three parts of an inch; then, let me tell thee, that my vengeance will fetch a great premium *here!*"

"He smites his chest," whispered Stubb, "what's that for? It rings most vast but hollow."

"Vengeance on a dumb brute!" cried Starbuck, "that simply smote thee from blindest instinct! Madness! To be enraged with a dumb thing, Captain Ahab, seems blasphemous."

"That inscrutable thing is chiefly what I hate; be the white whale agent, or be the white whale principal, I will wreak that hate upon him. Talk not to me of blasphemy, man; I'd strike the sun if it insulted me. But look ye, Starbuck, what is said in heat, that thing unsays itself. There are men from whom warm words are small indignity. I meant not to incense thee. Let it go. The crew, man, the crew! Are they not one and all with Ahab, in this matter of the whale?"

"God keep me!—keep us all!" murmured Starbuck, lowly.

Chapter 23. Sunset

The cabin; by the stern windows; Ahab sitting alone, and gazing out.

I, Ishmael, was one of that crew; my shouts had gone up with the rest; my oath had been welded with theirs; strong I shouted because of the dread in my soul. A wild, mystical, sympathetical feeling was in me; Ahab's quenchless feud seemed mine. With greedy ears, I learned the history of that murderous monster against whom we had taken our oaths of violence and revenge.

For some time, the unaccompanied, secluded White Whale had haunted those uncivilized seas mostly frequented by the Sperm Whale fishermen. But not all of them knew of his existence.

One of the wild suggestions in the minds of the superstitiously inclined, was the unearthly conceit that Moby Dick was ubiquitous; that he had actually been encountered in opposite latitudes at one and the same instant of time.

Once three boats circled around him; one captain, seizing the knife from his broken bow, had dashed at the whale, as an Arkansas duellist[130] at his foe, blindly seeking with a six-inch blade to reach the fathom-deep life of the whale. That captain was Ahab. And then it was, that Moby Dick had reaped away Ahab's leg, as a mower a blade of grass in the field.

There's no wonder that ever since that almost fatal encounter, Ahab had cherished a wild vindictiveness against the whale, and in his frantic morbidness, he came to identify with him, not only all his bodily woes but all his intellectual and spiritual exasperations.

The White Whale swam before him as the monomaniac incarnation of all those malicious agencies which some deep men feel eating in them, till they are left living on with half a heart and half a lung. Ahab did not fall down and worship it like them, but deliriously transferring its idea to the abhorred white whale, he pitted himself, all mutilated, against it.

---

130 In the early 1800's duelling was a popular means of settling disputes, especially among political foes. Melville may have been referring to the 1827 duel between the Arkansas Governor and a Congressman. The Governor, having been called a liar, publicly by the Congressman, summoned for a duel. The Governor fired first, but only grazed the Congressman. The Congressman shot and killed the Governor.

All that most maddens and torments; all that stirs up the residue of things; all truth with malice in it; all that cracks the sinews and cakes the brain; all the subtle demonisms of life and thought; all evil, to crazy Ahab, were visibly personified, and made practically assailable in Moby Dick. He piled upon the whale's white hump the sum of all the general rage and hate felt by his whole race from Adam down.

That it was only then, on the homeward voyage, after the encounter, that the final mania seized him, at intervals during the passage, he was a raving lunatic; and, though unlimbed of a leg, yet such vital strength yet lurked in his Egyptian chest and was moreover intensified by his delirium, that his mates were forced to tie him up, even there, as he sailed, raving in his hammock. In a strait-jacket, he swung to the mad rockings of the waves.

And, when running into more sufferable seas, the ship floated across the tranquil tropics, and, to all appearances, the old man's delirium seemed left behind him, and he came forth from his dark den into the blessed light and air; even then, when he bore that firm, collected front, and issued his calm orders once again; and his mates thanked God the direful madness was now gone; even then, Ahab, in his hidden self, raved on. Human madness is oftentimes a cunning and most feline thing. When you think it fled, it may have but become transfigured into some still subtler form. Ahab's full lunacy subsided not but deepeningly contracted. Far from having lost his strength, Ahab did now possess a thousandfold more potency.

Ahab had purposely sailed upon the present voyage with the one only and all-engrossing object of hunting the White Whale. He was intent on audacious and supernatural revenge.

Here, then, was this grey-headed, ungodly old man, chasing with curses a Job's whale around the world at the head of a crew, chiefly made up of mongrel renegades, and castaways, and cannibals, by the right-minded Starbuck, the indifference and recklessness in Stubb, and the pervading mediocrity in Flask. Such a crew seemed specially picked and packed by some infernal fatality to help him in his manic revenge. How it was that they so aboundingly responded to the old man's ire—by what evil magic their souls were possessed, that at times his hate seemed almost theirs; the White Whale as much their insufferable foe as his; how all this came to be—what the White Whale was to them, or how to their unconscious understandings, in some unsuspected way, he might have seemed the great demon of the seas of life,—all this to explain, would be to dive deeper than Ishmael can go.

Chapter 24. There She Blows

What the white whale was to Ahab has been said; what, at times, he was to me, as yet remains a mystery.

It was the whiteness of the whale that, above all things, appalled me. But how can I hope to explain myself here; and yet, in some dim, random way, explain myself I must, else all these chapters might be naught.

Though in many natural objects, whiteness enhances beauty, as if imparting some special virtue of its own, as in marbles and pearls. White is specially employed in the celebration of the Passion of our Lord; and the Holy One that sitteth there white like wool; yet for all these accumulated associations, with whatever is sweet, and honorable, and sublime, there yet lurks an elusive something in the innermost idea of this hue, which strikes more of panic to the soul than that redness which affrights in blood.

In the solitude of his cabin, Ahab pondered over his charts. Almost every night, they were brought out; almost every night, some pencil marks were erased, and others were substituted.

Now, to anyone not fully acquainted with the ways of the leviathans[131], it might seem an absurdly hopeless task thus to seek out one solitary creature in the unending oceans of this planet. But to Ahab, who knew the sets of all tides and currents; and thereby calculating the driftings of the sperm whale's food; and, also, calling to mind the regular, ascertained seasons for hunting him in particular latitudes; could arrive at reasonable surmises, almost approaching to certainties, concerning the timeliest day to be upon this or that ground in search of his prey.

Besides, when making a passage from one feeding ground to another, the sperm whales, guided by some infallible instinct—rather, secret intelligence from the Deity—mostly swim in *veins*, as they are called; continuing their way along a given ocean-line with

---

131 Leviathan is a mythical sea creature, symbolically used in the bible as a great enemy. The usage by Herman Melville set a course that evolved the modern usage of the term to also mean A Great Whale.

such undeviating exactitude, that no ship ever sailed her course, with one tithe[132] of such marvelous precision.

Having impulsively and perhaps somewhat prematurely revealed the prime but private purpose of the Pequod's voyage, Ahab was now entirely conscious that, in so doing, he had indirectly laid himself open to the unanswerable charge of usurpation[133]; and with perfect impunity, both moral and legal, his crew if so disposed could refuse all further obedience to him, and even violently wrest from him the command.

For all these reasons, Ahab plainly saw that he must still in a good degree continue true to the natural, nominal purpose of the Pequod's voyage; and not only that but force himself to funnel all his well known passionate interest in the general pursuit of his profession.

It was a cloudy, sultry afternoon; the seamen were lazily lounging about the decks, when I heard a sound so strange, long-drawn, and musically wild and unearthly, that the ball of free will dropped from my hand, and I stood gazing up at the clouds whence that voice dropped like a wing.

To be sure, the same sound was that very moment being heard all over the seas, from hundreds of whalemen's look-outs perched as high in the air; but from few of those lungs could that accustomed old cry have derived such a marvelous cadence as from Tashtego the Indian's.

"There she blows! There! There! There! she blows! she blows!"

"Where-away?"

"On the lee-beam, about two miles off! a school of them!"

Instantly all was a commotion.

"There go flukes!" was now the cry from Tashte, and the whales disappeared.

---

132 Typically a tithe refers to one tenth of one's income. Melville was known, according to what remains of his journals, to visit various churches and if he felt that the preacher was tolerable, offering mercy instead of hammering justice, he would often pay a tithe before leaving. Melville never realized wealth from Moby Dick or any of his other works and died poor. So, 1/10th of his income, would have been very little, a widow's mite.

133 Using his power as captain for his own selfish purposes.

Chapter 25. The Spirit-Spout

Days, weeks passed, and under easy sail, the ivory Pequod slowly swept across four cruising-grounds. Walking the deck with quick, side-lunging strides, Ahab commanded the sails. And had you watched Ahab's face that night, you would have thought he was at war. While his one live leg made lively echoes along the deck, every stroke of his dead limb sounded like a coffin-tap. On life and death, this old man walked.

During all this blackness of the elements, Ahab, though assuming for the time the almost continual command of the drenched and dangerous deck, manifested the gloomiest reserve; and more seldom than ever addressed his mates.

In tempestuous times like these, after everything above and aloft has been secured, nothing more can be done but passively to await the issue of the gale. So, with his ivory leg inserted into its accustomed hole and with one hand firmly grasping a shroud, Ahab for hours and hours would stand gazing dead to windward, while an occasional squall of sleet or snow would all but seal his very eyelashes together. Few or no words were spoken among the crew, and the silent ship, as if manned by painted sailors in wax, day after day tore on through all the swift madness and gladness of the demonic waves.

Starbuck could never forget the old man's purpose. Terrible old man! Thought Starbuck with a shudder, sleeping in this bunk, still steadfastly eyest thy purpose.

Chapter 26. Pandemic

H and in hand, ship, and breeze blew on, but the breeze came faster than the ship, and soon the Pequod began to rock.

The ships of the American Whale Fleet each have a private signal; which are collected in a book with the names of the respective vessels attached, every captain is provided with it.

The Pequod's signal was at last responded to by the stranger's setting her own, which proved the ship to be the Jeroboam of Nantucket.

As soon as it was identified, Stubb exclaimed—"That's he! That's he!" Stubb here alluded to a strange story told of the Jeroboam and a certain man among her crew.

He had been originally nurtured among the crazy society of Neskyeuna Shakers[134], where he had been a great prophet; in their cracked, secret meetings having several times descended from heaven by way of a trap-door, announcing the speedy opening of the seventh vial, which he carried in his vest-pocket; but, which, instead of containing gunpowder, was supposed to be charged with laudanum[135]. A strange, apostolic whim having seized him, he had left Neskyeuna for Nantucket, where, with that cunning peculiar to craziness, he assumed a steady, common-sense exterior and offered himself as a green-hand candidate for the Jeroboam's whaling voyage. They engaged him, but straightway upon the ship's getting out of sight of land, his insanity broke out in a flood. He announced himself as the archangel Gabriel[136]and commanded the captain to jump overboard.

---

134 The Shaker movement was at its height when Melville was working on Moby Dick. Nicknamed "the shaking quakers" for their enthusiastic worship style, they were also the first in modern Christianity to value women equal to men in leadership. Their followers were called to forsake marriage and live a celibate life as Adam's original sin was sex. The first colony of Shakers was established in Neskyeuna, Massachusetts.

135 In the 1800's laudanum was a medicine used to relieve pain and induce sleep. It was said to be "mixed with everything" and a "cure for every ailment." Its contents included opium, morphine, mercury, wine, whiskey, cayenne pepper, chloroform and ether."

136 Gabriel is known as the "message bearing" angel in the bible. He announced to the Virgin Mary that she was chosen to bear Jesus. Luke 1:19.

Gabriel was sacred in the minds of the majority of the ignorant crew. Moreover, they were afraid of him. He was not of much practical use in the ship, especially as he refused to work except when he pleased, the incredulous captain would loved to have been rid of him; but apprised of this intention, the archangel opened all his seals and vials—devoting the ship and all hands to unconditional perdition, in case this intention was carried out. So strongly did he work upon his disciples among the crew that at last they went to the captain and told him if Gabriel was sent from the ship, not a man of them would remain.

He was therefore forced to relinquish his plan. Nor would they permit Gabriel to be in any way maltreated, say, or do what he would so that it came to pass that Gabriel had the complete freedom of the ship. The consequence of all this was that the archangel cared little or nothing for the captain and mates; and since the epidemic had broken out, he carried a higher hand than ever; declaring that the plague, as he called it, was at his sole command; and would be around as long as he wanted.

The sailors, mostly poor devils, cringed in obedience to his instructions, sometimes rendering him personal homage, as to a god. Such things may seem incredible, but, however wondrous, they are true. This fanatic had not only measureless power to deceive and bedevil so many others, but he also deceived himself. But it is time to return to the Pequod.

She bore down and lowered a boat to accommodate the visiting captain, the stranger waved his hand from his boat's stern in token of that being entirely unnecessary. It turned out that the Jeroboam had a malignant epidemic[137] on board, and that Mayhew, her captain, was fearful of infecting the Pequod's company.

But this did by no means prevent all communications. Preserving an interval of some few yards between itself and the ship, a conversation was sustained between the two parties.

"I fear not thy epidemic, man," said Ahab from the bulwarks to Captain Mayhew, who stood in the boat's stern; "come on board."

But now Gabriel started to his feet.

"Think, think of the fevers, yellow and bilious! Beware of the horrible plague!"

---

137 Melville is likely referencing the mid 19th century cholera epidemic that started in Russia and killed over 1 million people. Cholera was transmitted along the California, Oregon and Mormon trails and it is believed that over 150,000 Americans died of Cholera between 1832 and 1849.

At that instant, a headlong wave shot the boat far ahead, drowning all speech.

"Hast thou seen the White Whale?" demanded Ahab when the boat drifted back.

Nothing was said for some moments while a succession of riotous waves rolled by.

When this interlude was over, Captain Mayhew began a dark story concerning Moby Dick, not, however, without frequent interruptions from Gabriel.

He said that the Jeroboam was told of the existence of Moby Dick and the havoc he had made. But Gabriel solemnly warned the captain against attacking the White Whale, in case the monster should be seen; in his gibbering insanity, pronouncing the White Whale to be no less than the Shaker God[138] incarnate.

But when, a year or two later, Moby Dick was sighted from the mast-heads, Macey, the chief mate, burned with a strong desire to encounter him; and the captain himself unwilling to let him have the opportunity, despite all the archangel's denunciations and forewarnings, Macey succeeded in persuading five men to man his boat. With them, he pushed off, and, after much weary pulling, and many perilous, unsuccessful attempts, he at last succeeded in getting one iron fast. Meantime, Gabriel, ascending to the main-royal mast-head, was tossing one arm in frantic gestures and hurling forth prophecies of speedy doom to the sacrilegious assailants of his divinity.

Now, while Macey, the mate, was standing up in his boat's bow, and with all the reckless energy of his tribe was venting his wild exclamations upon the whale and attempting to get a fair shot with his poised lance, lo! a broad white shadow rose from the sea; by its quick, fanning motion, temporarily taking the breath out of the bodies of the oarsmen. The next instant, the luckless mate, so full of furious life, was smitten bodily into the air, and making a long arc in his descent, fell into the sea at the distance of about fifty yards. Not a chip of the boat was harmed, nor a hair of any oarsman's head, but the mate forever sank.

The whole calamity, with the falling form of Macey, was plainly seen from the ship. Raising a piercing shriek—"The vial! the vial!" Gabriel called off the terror-stricken crew from the further hunting of the whale. This terrible event clothed the archangel with added influence;

---

138 Shakers believe that God was both male and female, that Jesus was the first male resurrection and their prophetess Ann Lee was the first female resurrection. Ann Lee brought the sect from England to the American colonies. She had frequent revelations and worked miracles, including healing the sick.

because his credulous disciples believed that he had specifically fore-announced it, instead of only making a general prophecy, which anyone might have done, and so have chanced to hit one of many marks in the wide margin allowed. He became a nameless terror to the ship.

Ahab made his intention known of hunting the White Whale if the opportunity preseented itself. Gabriel once more stood to his feet, glared upon the old man, and vehemently exclaimed, with downward pointed finger—"Think, think of the blasphemer—dead, and down there!—beware of the blasphemer's end!"

Chapter 27. Jonah

Reference was made to the historical story of Jonah and the whale in a preceding chapter. Now, some Nantucketers rather distrust this historical story of Jonah and the whale. But then there were some skeptical Greeks and Romans, who, standing out from the orthodox pagans of their times, equally doubted the story of Hercules and the whale, and Arion and the dolphin; and yet their doubting those traditions did not make those traditions one whit the less real, for all that.

Chapter 28. Vapor of Doubt

For six thousand years[139]—and no one knows how many millions of ages before—the great whales have been spouting all over the sea and sprinkling and mystifying the gardens of the deep, and for some centuries back, thousands of hunters have been close by the fountain of the whale, watching these sprinklings and spoutings, yet it still remains a problem, whether these spoutings are, after all, real water, or nothing but a vapor—this is surely a noteworthy thing.

In man, breathing is incessantly going on—one breath only serving for two or three pulsations; so that whatever other business he has to attend to, waking or sleeping, breathe he must, or die he will. But the Sperm Whale only breathes about one-seventh or Sunday of his time.

Still, we can hypothesize, even if we cannot prove and establish. My hypothesis is this: that the spout is nothing but mist. I am impelled to this conclusion by considerations of the great inherent dignity of the Sperm Whale; I account him no common, shallow being. I am convinced that from the heads of all ponderous profound beings, such as Plato, Pyrrho, the Devil, Jupiter, Dante, and so on, there always goes up to certain semi-visible steam, while in the act of thinking deep thoughts.

And how nobly it raises our conceit of the mighty, misty monster, to behold him solemnly sailing through a calm tropical sea; his vast, mild head overhung by a canopy of vapor, engendered by his contemplations, and that vapor—as you will sometimes see it—glorified by a rainbow, as if Heaven itself had put its seal upon his thoughts. Don't you see, rainbows do not visit the clear air; they only irradiate vapor. And so, through all the thick mists of the dim doubts in my mind, divine intuitions now and then shoot, arousing my fog with a heavenly ray. And for this I thank God; for all have doubts; many deny; but doubts or denials, few along with them, have intuitions. Doubts of all things earthly, and intuitions of some things heavenly; this combination makes neither believer nor infidel but makes a man who regards them both with an equal eye.

---

139 Young earth creationists believe that Adam and Eve were born six thousand years ago when the earth was created. Here, Melville, sarcastically highlights the audacious and uneducated claim.

Chapter 29. Smell

It was a week or two after the last whaling scene recounted, and when we were slowly sailing over a sleepy, vapory, mid-day sea, that the many noses on the Pequod's deck smelled a peculiar and not very pleasant smell.

"I will bet something now," said Stubb, "that somewhere here are some of those drugged whales we tickled the other day. I thought they would keel up before long."

There in the distance lay a ship whose furled sails indicated that some sort of whale must be alongside. As we glided nearer, the stranger showed French colors from his peak. It was clear that the whale alongside must be what the fishermen call a blasted whale, that is, a whale that has died unmolested on the sea, and so floated as an unclaimed corpse. Such an unsavory odor was worse than an Assyrian[140] city in the plague, when the living is incompetent to bury the departed.

Coming still nearer with the expiring breeze, we saw that the Frenchman had a second whale alongside; and this second whale seemed even more scented than the first. In truth, it turned out to be one of those problematic whales that seem to dry up and die with a sort of prodigious dyspepsia or indigestion, leaving their defunct bodies almost entirely bankrupt of anything like oil.

The Pequod had now swept so close to the stranger that Stubb vowed he recognized his harpoon entangled in the lines that were knotted round the tail of one of these whales.

"There's a pretty fellow, now," he banteringly laughed, standing in the ship's bows, "there's a jackal for you! I well know that these Crappo[141] Frenchmen are but poor devils in the fishery; sometimes lowering their boats for breakers[142], mistaking them for Sperm Whale spouts; yes, and sometimes sailing from their port with their hold full of boxes of tallow

---

140 The failure of the Assyrians to capture and overtake Jerusalem is one of the "baffling" episodes in the bible as they were powerful and known for their might and cruelty. One theory, based on ancient writings, is that the Assyrian army was decimated by an infestation of the rat borne bubonic plague.

141 A derogatory nautical term for a French sailor.

142 A breaking wave or breaker can have the look of a whale spouting vapor, especially to untrained eyes.

candles[143], and cases of snuffers[144], foreseeing that all the oil they will get won't be enough to dip the Captain's wick into. And as for the other whale, why, I'll agree to get more oil by chopping up and trying out these three masts of ours than he'll get from that bundle of bones."

By this time, the faint air had become a complete calm; the Pequod was now fairly entrapped in the smell, with no hope of escaping except by its sailing again. Issuing from the cabin, Stubb now prepared to call his boat's crew to pull off from the French stranger.

Now in order to hold direct communication with the people on deck, he had to pull around the bows to the starboard side and thus come close to the blasted whale; and so talk over it.

Arriving then at this spot, with one hand still to his nose, he bawled—"Ahoy! are there any of you that speak English?"

"Yes," rejoined a Guernsey-man from the bulwarks, who turned out to be the chief-mate.

"Well, then, my bud, have you seen the White Whale?"

"*What* whale?"

"The *White* Whale—a Sperm Whale—Moby Dick, have ye seen him?

"Never heard of such a whale. Cachalot Blanche! White Whale—no."

"Very good, then; good bye now, and I'll call again in a minute."

Then rapidly pulling back towards the Pequod, and seeing Ahab leaning over the quarter-deck rail awaiting his report, he molded his two hands into a trumpet and shouted—"No, Sir! No!" Upon which Ahab retired.

---

143 A small bedside candle made of the hard fat of an animal or whale.

144 A candle extinguisher.

Chapter 30. An Arm and a Leg

"Ship, ahoy! Have you seen the White Whale?"

So cried Ahab, once more hailing a ship showing English colors, bearing down under the stern.

"Have you seen the White Whale?"

"Look here!" and withdrawing it from the folds that had hidden it, the English Captain held up a white arm of sperm whale bone, terminating in a wooden head like a mallet.

"Man, my boat!" cried Ahab impetuously, and tossing about the oars near him—"Stand by to lower!"

In less than a minute, he and his crew were dropped to the water and were soon alongside the stranger.

Soon he was carefully swung inside the ship and gently landed upon the ground. With his ivory arm frankly thrust forth in welcome, the English captain advanced, and Ahab, putting out his ivory leg and crossing the ivory arm (like two sword-fish blades), cried out in his walrus way, "Aye, aye, hearty! Let us shake bones together!—an arm and a leg!—an arm that never can shrink, d'ye see; and a leg that never can run. Where did you see the White Whale?—how long ago?"

"The White Whale," said the Englishman, pointing his ivory arm towards the East as if it had been a telescope; "there I saw him, on the Line, last season."

"And he took that arm off, did he?" asked Ahab, resting on the Englishman's shoulder.

"Aye, he was the cause of it, at least, and that leg, too?"

"It was he, it was he!" cried Ahab, suddenly letting out his suspended breath.

"And harpoons sticking in near his starboard fin."

"Aye, aye—they were mine— my irons," cried Ahab triumphantly.

"What became of the White Whale?" now asked Ahab.

"Oh!" cried the one-armed captain, "oh, yes! Well; we didn't see him again for some time; in fact, as I before hinted, I didn't then know what whale it was that had served me such a trick, till some time afterward, when coming back to the Line, we heard about Moby Dick—as some call him—and then I knew it was he."

"Did you see him again?"

"Twice."

"But you didn't kill him?"

"Didn't want to try to: ain't one limb enough? What should I do without this other arm? And I'm thinking Moby Dick doesn't bite so much as he swallows."

"No, thank you, said the English Captain, "he's welcome to the arm he has, since I can't help it, and didn't know him then, but not to another one. No more White Whales for me; I've lowered for him once, and that has satisfied me. There would be great glory in killing him, I know that, and there is a ship-load of precious sperm in him, but, I believe, he's best let alone; don't you think so, Captain?"—glancing at the ivory leg.

"He is. But he will still be hunted. What is best left alone often allures the most. How long since you saw him last? Which way was he heading?"

"Good God!" cried the English Captain, to whom the question was put. "What's the matter? He was heading east, I think.—Is your Captain crazy?"

But Ahab commanded the ship's sailors to stand by to lower.

In a moment, he was standing in the boat's stern, and the Manilla men were springing to their oars. In vain, the English Captain hailed him. With back to the stranger ship and face set like a flint to his own, Ahab stood upright till alongside the Pequod.

Chapter 31. Ahab's Leg

The sudden manner in which Captain Ahab left the Samuel Enderby[145] of London caused some small violence to his own person. He had swooped down with such energy to the deck that his ivory leg received a half-splintering shock. And when after landing his own deck, and his own pivot-hole there, he so vehemently wheeled round with an urgent command to the steersman; that the already shaken ivory received such an additional twist and wrench, that Ahab did not deem it entirely trustworthy.

For all his mad recklessness, Ahab did at times give careful heed to the condition of that dead bone upon which he partly stood.

For Ahab both the ancestry and posterity of Grief go further than the ancestry and posterity of Joy. For, thought Ahab, even the highest earthly eloquence has pettiness lurking in it. Even the Gods themselves are not forever glad.

Whatever the unseen ambiguous counsel in the air or the vindictive princes of fire have to do with earthly Ahab, yet, in this present matter of his leg, he took plain practical procedures;—he called the carpenter[146].

And when the carpenter appeared before him, he bade him without delay to set about making a new leg and directed the mates to see him supplied with all the studs and joists of jaw-ivory (Sperm Whale) which had thus far been accumulated on the voyage, in order that a careful selection of the stoutest, clearest-grained stuff might be secured.

This done, the carpenter received orders to have the leg completed that night.

---

145 Samuel Enderby was an English whale oil merchant, significant in the history of whaling in the United Kingdom.

146 Mark 6:3 "Then they scoffed; He's just a carpenter, the son of Mary and the brother of James, Joseph, Judas, and Simon. And his sisters live right here among us. They were deeply offended and refused to believe in him."

Chapter 32. The Carpenter

Seat thyself among the moons of Saturn and take high abstracted man alone, and he seems a wonder. But from the same point, take mankind in mass, and for the most part, they seem a mob of unnecessary duplicates. But most humble though he was the Pequod's carpenter was no duplicate.

Like all sea-going ship carpenters, and more especially those belonging to whaling vessels, he was experienced in numerous trades and callings collateral to his own. Along with woodwork, this carpenter of the Pequod was also efficient in the thousand nameless mechanical emergencies continually recurring in a large ship.

Was it that this old carpenter had been a life-long wanderer, whose much rolling, to and fro, rubbed off whatever warts clung to him? He was a naked abstract, an unfractioned integral, uncompromised as a new-born babe, living without premeditated reference to this world or the next. He did not seem to work so much by reason or by instinct, or simply because he had been tutored to it, or by any combination of all these, but merely by a kind of deaf and dumb, spontaneous literal process. He was a pure manipulator; his brain, if he had ever had one, must have early oozed along into the muscles of his fingers.

"Look here carpenter", Ahad said to him. "You call yourself good? Well, then, when I come to mount this leg thou makest, I shall nevertheless feel another leg in the same identical place with it; that is, carpenter, my old lost leg; the flesh and blood one, I mean. Canst thou not drive that old Adam away?"

"Look, put thy live leg in the place where mine once was; so nowhere is only one distinct leg to the eye, yet two to the soul. Where thou feelest tingling life; there, exactly there, do I. And if I still feel the pain of my crushed leg, though it is now so long dissolved, then why mayest, not thou, carpenter, feel the fiery pains of hell forever, and without a body?"

"Oh, Life! Here I am, proud as a Greek god and yet standing debtor to this blockhead for a bone to stand on! Cursed be that mortal inter-indebtedness which will not do away with debt. I would be free as air."

CARPENTER (*resuming his work*).

Chapter 33. Leaking Oil

They were pumping the ship the next morning, and Lo! A considerable amount of oil came up with the water; the casks[147] must have sprung a bad leak. Starbuck went down into the cabin to report this unfavorable affair to Ahab.

On a whaleboat, with oil on board, it is a regular semiweekly duty to drench the casks with seawater which afterward is removed by the ship's pumps. The mariners can readily detect any serious leakage in the precious cargo.

Starbuck found Ahab with a general chart of the oriental archipelagoes spread before him; and another separate one representing the long eastern coasts of the Japanese islands.

"Who's there?" hearing the footstep at the door but not turning round to it.

"Captain Ahab; it is I. The oil in the hold is leaking, sir. We must pack up and break out."

"Pack up and break out" Now that we are nearing Japan?"

"Either do that, sir, or waste in one day more oil than we may make in a good year. What we come twenty thousand miles to get is worth saving, sir."

"Begone! Let it leak! I'm all a leak myself. Yet, I don't stop to plug my leak. Starbuck! I will not turn around."

"What will the owners say, sir?"

"Let the owners stand on Nantucket beach and out yell the Typhoons[148]. What do I care? Owners, owners? As if the owners were my conscience. But look, the only real owner of anything is its commander; and listen, my conscience is in this ship's keel. On deck!"

---

147 Large, barrel like containers holding the whale oil.

148 In modern terms, "They can go pound sand."

"Captain Ahab," said the reddening mate, moving further into his cabin, with a daring so strangely respectful and cautious. "A better man than I might well resent you, Captain Ahab."

"Devils! Do you dare think so critically of me?—On deck!"

"No, sir, not yet; Shall we not try to understand each other better, Captain Ahab?"

Ahab seized a loaded musket from the rack and, pointing it towards Starbuck, exclaimed: "There is one God that is Lord over the earth, and one Captain that is lord over the Pequod.—On deck!"

For an instant in the flashing eyes of the mate and his fiery cheeks, you would have almost thought that he had really received the blaze of the leveled tube. But, mastering his emotion, he half calmly rose, and as he left the cabin, paused for an instant and said: "You have outraged, not insulted me, sir; but for that, I ask you not to beware of Starbuck; but let Ahab beware of Ahab; beware of thyself, old man."

"He waxes brave but nevertheless obeys!" murmured Ahab, as Starbuck disappeared. "What's that he said—Ahab beware of Ahab—there's something there!" Then unconsciously using the musket for a staff, he paced to and fro in the little cabin; soon the thick folds of his forehead relaxed, and returning the gun to the rack, he went to the deck.

"Thou art but too good a fellow, Starbuck," he said lowly to the mate, then raising his voice to the crew: "Furl the t'gallant-sails, and close-reef the top-sails, fore and aft; back the main-yard; pack up, and turn around."

It was perhaps vain to surmise exactly why it was, that as respecting Starbuck, Ahab thus acted. It may have been a flash of honesty in him. However it was, his orders were executed.

Chapter 34. Queequeg in His Coffin

Upon searching, it was found that the casks were perfectly sound and that the leak must be further off. So with the calm weather, they broke out deeper and deeper.

Now, at this time, my poor pagan companion, and fast bosom-friend, Queequeg, was seized with a fever, which brought him close to his endless end. Stripped down to his woolen drawers, the tattooed savage was crawling about amid the dampness and slime, and for all the heat of his sweating, he caught a terrible chill which lapsed into a fever and at last, after some days' suffering, laid him in his hammock, close to the very door of death.

How he wasted and wasted away in those few long-lingering days, till there seemed but little left of him but his frame and tattooing. But as all else in him thinned, and his cheekbones grew sharper, his eyes, nevertheless, seemed growing full and fuller, they became a strange softness of luster; and mildly but deeply looked out at you there from his sickness, a wondrous testimony to that immortal health in him which could not die, or be weakened.

His eyes seemed rounding and rounding, like the rings of Eternity. An awe that cannot be named would steal over you as you sat by the side of this waning savage. For whatever is truly wondrous and fearful in man, never yet was put into words or books. And the drawing near of Death, which levels all alike, impresses all with a last revelation, which only an author from the dead could adequately tell.

So that, let us say it again, no dying Greek had higher and holier thoughts than those, whose mysterious shades you saw creeping over the face of poor Queequeg, as he quietly lay in his swaying hammock, and the rolling sea seemed gently rocking him to his final rest, and the ocean's invisible flood-tide lifted him higher and higher towards his destined heaven.

Not a man of the crew gave up on him, and, as for Queequeg himself, what he thought was shown by a curious favor he asked. He called me to him, and taking his hand, said that while in Nantucket he saw certain little canoes of dark wood; and had learned that all whalemen who died in Nantucket were laid in those same dark canoes.

He added that he shuddered at the thought of being buried in his hammock. He desired a canoe like those of Nantucket.

Now, when this strange request was given, the carpenter was at once commanded to do Queequeg's bidding, whatever it might be.

When the last nail was driven and the lid fitted, he lightly shouldered the coffin and went forward with it, inquiring whether they were ready for it yet in that direction. Queequeg, to every one's surprise, asked that the thing should be instantly brought to him. He then called for his harpoon and biscuits and a flask of freshwater. Queequeg now asked to be lifted into his final bed, that he might test its comfort.

But now that he had apparently made every preparation for death; now that his coffin was proved a good fit, Queequeg suddenly rallied; at this critical moment, he had just recalled a little duty ashore, which he had left undone; and therefore had changed his mind about dying: he could not die yet, he said. They asked him, then, whether to live or die was a matter of his own sovereign will and pleasure. He answered, certainly. In a word, it was Queequeg's opinion that if a man made up his mind to live, mere sickness could not kill him: nothing but a whale, or a gale, or some violent, ungovernable destroyer of that sort.

Now, there is this noteworthy difference between savage and civilized; that while a sick, civilized man may be six months recovering, generally speaking, a sick savage is almost half-well again in a day. So, in good time my Queequeg gained strength; and at length, after sitting on the deck for a few idle days (but eating with a vigorous appetite,) he suddenly leaped to his feet, threw out his arms and legs, gave himself a good stretching, yawned a little bit, and then springing into the head of his hoisted boat, and poising a harpoon, pronounced himself fit for a fight.

With a wild whimsiness, he now used his coffin for a sea-chest, and emptying into it his canvas bag of clothes, set them in order there. Many spare hours he spent, in carving the lid with all manner of grotesque figures and drawings; and it seemed that he was striving to copy parts of the twisted tattooing on his body. And this tattooing had been the work of a departed prophet and seer of his island, who, by those hieroglyphic marks, had written out on his body a complete theory of the heavens and the earth and a mystical treatise on the art of attaining truth.

But whose mysteries not even he could read, though his own live heart beat against them.

Chapter 35. The Castaway

In a whale ship, not everyone goes in the boats. Those called ship-keepers work the vessel while the boats are pursuing the whale. In general, these ship-keepers are as hardy fellows as the men comprising the boats' crews. But if there happens to be an unduly slender or clumsy creature in the ship, that sailor is certain to be made a ship-keeper. It was so in the Pequod with the little black boy Pippin, by nickname, Pip by abbreviation. Poor Pip! Pip loved life and all life's peaceable securities.

When Stubb's oarsman sprained his hand, Pip was temporarily put into his place.

The first time Stubb lowered with him, Pip was nervous, but thankfully, for that time escaped close contact with the whale and came off credible. On the second lowering, the boat paddled upon the whale, and as the fish received the darted iron, it gave its customary rap, which happened to be right under poor Pip's seat. This caused him to leap out of the boat, paddle in hand, and in such a way, that part whale line became entangled in his chest.

The instant the stricken whale started on a fierce run, the line swiftly straightened, and presto! Poor Pip came all foaming up to the deck of the boat, terrifyingly dragged there by the line, which had taken several turns around his chest and neck.

Tashtego stood in the bows. He hated Pip for distracting them from the chase. Snatching the knife from its sheath, he suspended its sharp edge over the line, and turning towards Stubb, exclaimed, "Cut?" Meantime Pip's blue, choked face cried out, Do for God's sake!

All time passed in a flash. In less than half a minute, this entire thing happened.

"Damn it, cut!" roared Stubb, and so the whale was lost, and Pip was saved.

As soon as he recovered himself, Pip was assailed by yells from the crew. Stubb concluded with a command, "Stick to the boat, Pip, or by the Lord. I won't pick you up anymore; mind that. We can't afford to lose whales by the likes of you; a whale would sell for thirty times what you would, Pip, in Alabama. Bear that in mind, and don't jump anymore."

But we are all in the hands of the Gods and Pip fell overboard again. It was under very similar circumstances to the first performance, but this time Pip was left behind in the sea. Alas! Stubb was but too true to his word. Bobbing up and down in that sea, Pip's ebony head showed like a head of cloves.

But had Stubb really abandoned Pip to his fate? No, he did not mean to, at least. Because there were two boats in his wake, and he supposed, no doubt, that they would, of course, come up to Pip very quickly. But it so happened that those boats, without seeing Pip, suddenly spying whales close to them on one side, turned, and gave chase.

By the merest chance, the Pequod itself at last rescued him, but from that hour, the little Pip was known as an idiot. The sea had kept his body up but drowned the infinite of his soul.

Not drowned entirely, though, rather carried down alive to wondrous depths, where Pip saw the multitudinous, god omnipresent. He saw God's foot upon the treadle[149] of the loom and spoke about it; therefore, his shipmates called him mad.

"The greatest idiot ever scolds the lesser," muttered Ahab, coming to deck. "Hands off from that holiness! Where sayest though Pip was?"

"Astern there, sir, astern!"

"Here, boy; Ahab's cabin shall be Pip's home from now on, while I live. You touch my inmost center, boy; thou art tied to me by cords woven of my heartstrings. Come with me."

Had poor Pip but felt so kind a thing as this, perhaps he never have been lost!

"Come then to my cabin. Lo! You believers in God's all goodness! See the omniscient Gods oblivious of suffering man; and man, though idiotic, and knowing not what he does, yet full of the sweet things of love and gratitude. Come! I feel prouder leading thee by thy black hand than though I grasped an Emperor's!"

---

149 A treadle loom is a sewing machine operated by a foot crank. The Critic James Wood said, "During the time that Melville wrote *Moby-Dick*, he underwent a kind of insanity of metaphor" hunting for meaning in all things that entered his mind. It is known that Melville's wife Lizzie had one of these sewing machines and Herman would sometimes bring her in a button to sew on to his coat. Much can be said about the metaphor of Pip seeing "God's foot upon the treadle of the loom". Pip had insight into God's handiwork and was being used as his instrument in one final attempt to save Ahab.

Chapter 36. Rachel

*T*he coffin laid upon two-line tubs, the carpenter caulking its seams. Ahab comes slowly from the cabin and hears Pip following him.

"What's here?"

"Life-buoy, sir. Mr. Starbuck's orders. I patched this thing here as a coffin for Queequeg, but they've set me now to turning it into something else."

Ahab to Himself

"Oh! How immaterial are all materials! What things real are there, but imponderable thoughts? A life-buoy of a coffin! Does it go further? Can it be that in some spiritual sense, the coffin is, after all, but an immortality-preserver! I'll think of that. So far gone am I in the dark side of the earth, that its other side, the theoretic bright one, seems but uncertain twilight to me. I go below; let me not see that thing here when I return again. Now, then, Pip, we'll talk this over; I do learn the most wondrous philosophies from you! Some unknown conduits from the unknown worlds must empty into you!"

The next day, a large ship, the Rachel was seen bearing directly down upon the Pequod.

"Hast seen the White Whale?" Ahab's voice was heard.

"Aye yesterday. And have ye seen a whale-boat adrift?"

Throttling his joy, Ahab negatively answered this unexpected question; and would then have fain boarded the stranger, when the stranger captain himself was seen descending her side. Immediately he was recognized by Ahab for a Nantucketer he knew. But no formal salutation was exchanged.

"Where was he? Not killed, not killed?" Cried Ahab.

It seemed that late on the afternoon of the previous day, the white hump and head of Moby Dick had suddenly come up out of the water, whereupon, a boat had been instantly lowered in chase. This boat seemed to have succeeded in harpooning the whale. Then a swift gleam of bubbling white water, and after that nothing more. It was concluded that the stricken whale must have run away with the boat, as often happens.

After the story was told, the Rachel's Captain immediately went on to reveal his object in boarding the Pequod. He desired that ship to unite with his own in the search.

"My boy, my own boy is among them. For God's sake, I beg, I plead, exclaimed the Captain to Ahab, who thus far icily received his petition. "I will gladly pay for it."

"His son!" cried Stubb, "oh, it's his son he's lost! Come on Ahab? We must save that boy."

Now, what made this incident of the Rachel's the more tragic, was among the boat's crew was a boy, a little lad, but twelve years old, whose father with the earnest hardiness of a Nantucker's paternal love, sent him to initiate him in the perils and wonders of this vocation. As often occurs, that Nantucket captains will send a son of such tender age away from them; so that their first knowledge of a whaleman's career shall be un-interfered with by any display of a father's natural but affection, or undue apprehensiveness and concern.

The stranger was still pleading his request to Ahab, and Ahab still stood like an anvil, receiving every shock, but without the least quivering of his own.

"I will not go," said the stranger, "till you say yes to me. Do to me as you would have me do to you in the like case[150]." For YOU too have a boy, Captain Ahab, though but a child, and nestling safely at home now. A child of your old age too.

"No," cried Ahab. "Captain Gardiner, I will not do it. Even now I lose time. Good-bye, good-bye. God bless ye, man, and may I forgive myself, but I must go."

Soon the two ships diverged their wakes, but by her still halting course and winding, woeful way, you plainly saw that this ship that so wept with spray, still remained without comfort. She was Rachel[151], weeping for her children, because they were not.

---

150 Matthew 25:40: "Verily I say unto you, Inasmuch as ye have done it unto one of the least of these my brethren, ye have done it unto me."

151 Rachel is one of the few biblical heroines. The mother of Joseph and Benjamin, two of the twelve tribes of Israel. When Rachel's children were lost in exile she "wept and refused to be comforted for her children, because they were not." Jeremiah 31: 15

Chapter 37. Soliloquy of Ahab

*A*hab moving to go on deck; Pip catches him by the hand to follow.

A "Lad, lad, I tell you not to follow Ahab now. The hour is coming[152] when Ahab would not push you away, yet would not have you by him. There is something in you, poor lad, which I feel is so curing to me."

"Listen, and you will often hear my ivory foot upon the deck, and still know that I am there. And now I leave you. You art true, lad, as the circumference to its center. So, God forever bless thee; and if it comes to that, God forever save thee, let what will come."

The Pequod sailed on; the rolling waves and days went by; the life-buoy-coffin still lightly swung. Slowly crossing the deck, Ahab leaned over the side and watched how his shadow in the water sank to his gaze. The lovely aromas in that enchanted air dispelled, for a moment, the cancerous thing in his soul. That glad, happy air stroked and caressed him; the step-mother world, so long cruel, forbidding, now threw affectionate arms around his stubborn neck, and joyously sobbed over him, however wilfully a sinner, she could yet find it in her heart to save and to bless.

From beneath his slouched hat Ahab dropped a tear into the sea, nor did all the Pacific contain such wealth as that one wee drop.

Starbuck saw the old man; saw him, how he heavily leaned over the side; and he seemed to hear in his own true heart the measureless sobbing that stole out of the center of the serenity around.

Careful not to touch him, or be noticed by him, he yet drew near to him, and stood there.

Ahab turned.

"Starbuck!"

---

152 John 5:25: "*The hour is coming*, and now is, when the dead shall hear the voice of the son of God; and those who hear will live.

"Sir."

"Oh, Starbuck! It is a mild, mild wind, and a mild looking sky. On such a day, very much such sweetness as this, I struck my first whale, a boy harpooner of eighteen! Forty, forty, forty years ago! Forty years of continual whaling! Forty years of privation, and peril, and storm time! Forty years on the pitiless sea! For forty years Ahab has forsaken the peaceful land, for forty years to make war on the horrors of the deep! Yes, Starbuck, out of those forty years I have not spent three ashore. When I think of this life I have led; the desolation of solitude it has been; the masoned walled town of a Captain's exclusiveness, which admits but small entrance to any sympathy from the green country without. Oh, weariness! Heaviness!

When I think of all this; whole oceans away, from that young girl-wife I wedded past fifty, and sailed for Cape Horn the next day, leaving but one dent in my marriage pillow—wife? wife?—rather a widow with her husband alive! Aye, I widowed that poor girl when I married her, Starbuck; and then, the madness, the frenzy, the boiling blood and the smoking brow, with which, for a thousand lowerings old Ahab has furiously, foamingly chased his prey—more a demon than a man!—aye, aye! what a forty years' fool—fool—old fool, has old Ahab been!

Why this strife of the chase? Why weary, and palsy the arm at the oar, and the iron, and the lance? How the richer or better is Ahab now? Behold. Oh, Starbuck! is it not hard, that with this weary load I bear, one poor leg should have been snatched from under me? Here, brush this old hair aside; it blinds me, that I seem to weep. Locks so grey, grown out from ashes! But do I look very old, so very, very old, Starbuck? I feel deadly faint, bowed, and humped, as though I were Adam, staggering beneath the piled centuries since Paradise. God! God! God!—crack my heart!—stave my brain!—mockery! mockery! bitter, biting mockery of grey hairs, have I lived enough joy to wear ye; and seem and feel thus intolerably old? Close! stand close to me, Starbuck; let me look into a human eye; it is better than to gaze into sea or sky; better than to gaze upon God. This is the magic glass; I see my wife and my child in your eye."

"Oh, my Captain! my Captain! noble soul! grand old heart, after all! Why should any one give chase to that hated fish! Away with me! let us fly these deadly waters! Let us go home! Wife and child, too, are Starbuck's—wife and child of his brotherly, sisterly, play-fellow youth; even as yours, sir, are the wife and child of your loving, longing, paternal old age! Away! let us leave!—this instant let me alter the course! How cheerily, how hilariously, O my Captain, would we boat on our way to see old Nantucket again! I think, sir, they have some such mild blue days, even as this, in Nantucket."

"They have, they have. I have seen them—some summer days in the morning. About this time—yes, it is his noon nap now—the boy vivaciously wakes; sits up in bed; and his mother tells him of me, of cannibal old me; how I am abroad upon the deep, but will yet come back to dance with him again."

"'Tis my Mary, my Mary herself! She promised that my boy, every morning, should be carried to the hill to catch the first glimpse of his father's sail! Yes, yes! no more! it is done! we head for Nantucket! Come, my Captain, study out the course, and let us leave! See, see! the boy's face from the window! the boy's hand on the hill!"

But Ahab's glance was averted; like a blighted fruit tree he shook, and cast his last, cindered[153] apple[154] to the soil.

"What is it, what nameless, inscrutable, unearthly thing is it; what hidden lord and master, and cruel, remorseless emperor commands me; that against all natural lovings and longings, I keep pushing; recklessly making me ready to do what in my own proper, natural heart, I don't so much as dare? Is Ahab, Ahab? Is it I, God, or who is it that lifts this arm?

But if the great sun move not of himself; but is as an errand-boy in heaven; nor one single star can revolve, but by some invisible power; how then can this one small heart beat; this one small brain think thoughts; unless God does that beating, does that thinking, does that living, and not I. By heaven, man, we are turned round and round in this world, by the wind and fate is our anchor.

But filled with despair, the Mate Starbuck left, sadly.

Ahab crossed the deck to gaze over on the other side; but stared at two reflected, fixed eyes in the water.

---

153 A mostly burned apple.

154 "Of Man's First Disobedience, and the Fruit Of that Forbidden Tree, whose mortal taste Brought Death into the World, and all our woe." Paradise Lost - John Milton.

Chapter 38. The Chase - The First Day

That night, in the mid-watch, when Ahab went to his pivot-hole, he suddenly thrust out his face fiercely, snuffing up the sea air as a ship's dog. He declared that a whale must be near. Soon that peculiar odor, given forth by the living sperm whale, was palpable to all at watch. Ahab rapidly ordered the ship's course to be slightly altered, and the sail to be shortened.

"Man the mast-heads! Call all hands!"

"What d'ye see?" cried Ahab, flattening his face to the sky.

"Nothing, nothing sir!" was the sound in reply.

All sail being set, he now cast loose the life-line and in a few moments they were hoisting him up and while peering ahead through the horizontal vacancy between the sails he raised a gull-like cry in the air.

"There she blows! There she blows! A hump like a snow-hill! It is Moby Dick!"

Ahab had now gained his final perch, some feet above the other lookouts.

"He is heading straight to leeward, sir," cried Stubb, "He's close to us; but hasn't seen the ship yet." Soon all the boats but Starbuck's were dropped, with Ahab heading the onset.

A gentle joy—a mighty mildness propelled the gliding whale.

Yet calm, enticing calm, oh, whale! thou glidest on, to all who for the first time see you.

And thus, through the serene tranquility of the tropical sea, Moby Dick moved on, still withholding from sight the full terrors of his submerged trunk, entirely hiding the wrenched hideousness of his jaw. But soon the front part of him slowly rose from the water; for an instant his whole marbleized body formed a high arch, like Virginia's Natural Bridge[155], and waving his tail in the air, the grand god revealed himself, sounded, and went out of sight.

The three boats now floated in silence, awaiting Moby Dick's reappearance.

Ahab could discover no sign in the sea. But suddenly as he peered down and down into its depths, he saw a small white living spot, with wonderful swiftness rising up, and magnifying as it rose, till it turned, and then there were plainly revealed two long crooked rows of white, glistening teeth, floating up from the undiscoverable bottom. It was Moby Dick's open mouth and scrolled jaw; his vast, shadowed bulk still half blending with the blue of the sea. The glittering mouth yawned beneath the boat like an open-doored marble tomb; and giving one sidelong sweep with his steering oar, Ahab whirled the craft aside from this tremendous apparition.

Then moving forward to the bows, and seizing a harpoon, commanded his crew to grasp their oars and stand by on deck.

But as if perceiving this strategy, Moby Dick, with that malicious intelligence ascribed to him, turned and shot his head lengthwise beneath the boat.

The whale lying on his back, in the manner of a biting shark, with its long, narrow, lower jaw curled high up into the open air, and one of the teeth caught in a row-lock[156]. The bluish pearl-white of the inside of the jaw was within six inches of Ahab's head, and reached higher than that. In this attitude the White Whale now shook the boat as a cruel cat her mouse.

As the whale dallied with the doomed craft in this devilish way, and before the boat was yet snapped, Ahab, the first to perceive the whale's intent, made one final effort to push the boat out of the bite. But only slipping further into the whale's mouth, and tilting over sideways as it slipped, the boat had shaken off his hold on the jaw; spilled him out of it; and so he fell flat-faced upon the sea.

---

155 A natural arched bridge in Virginia, worshipped by the Native Americans, purchased by Thomas Jefferson and surveyed by George Washington. It is now a popular recreational and tourist location.

156 The brace that attaches an oar to the boat.

Withdrawing from his prey, Moby Dick now lay at a little distance, swimming swiftly round and round the wrecked crew; sideways churning the water in his vengeful wake, as if preparing himself for another and more deadly assault.

The sight of the splintered boat seemed to madden him. Meanwhile Ahab half smothered in the foam of the whale's tail, and too much of a cripple to swim; floated.

The Pequod's bow was pointed; and breaking up the charmed circle, she effectively parted the white whale from his victim. As he sullenly swam off, the boats flew to the rescue.

Dragged into Stubb's boat with blood-shot, blinded eyes, Ahab's bodily strength did crack, and helplessly he yielded to his body's doom: for a time, lying all crushed in the bottom of Stubb's boat, like one trodden under foot of herds of elephants.

"My harpoon," said Ahab, half way rising, and leaning on one bended arm—"is it here?"

"Aye, sir, for it was not darted; this is it," said Stubb, showing it.

"That's good.—Help me, man; I wish to stand. So, so, I see him! There! There! going to leeward still; what a leaping spout!—Hands off from me! The eternal sap runs up in Ahab's bones again! Set the sail; out oars; the helm!"

It is often the case that when a boat and its crew is picked up by another boat, they help to work that second boat; and the chase is thus continued with what is called double-banked oars. It was thus now.

Then Ahab advancing towards the main mast "Men, this gold is mine, for I earned it; but I shall let it abide here till the White Whale is dead; and then, whosoever of ye first raises him, upon the day he shall be killed, this gold is that man's."

And after saying this, he placed himself half way within the cabin, and slouching his hat, stood there till dawn.

Chapter 39. The Chase - The Second Day

At day break, the harpoons were newly manned.

"D'ye see him?" cried Ahab after allowing a little space for the light to spread."

"See nothing, sir."

"Turn up all hands and make sail! He travels faster than I thought."

The ship tore on; leaving such a furrow in the sea. "There she blows, she blows! She blows! Right ahead!" was now the masthead cry.

"Aye, aye!" cried Stubb, "I knew it, you can't escape. Oh whale! The mad fiend himself is after you! And Stubb spoke for all the crew. Whatever fears some of them might have felt before, were kept out of sight through the growing awe of Ahab.

The hand of fate had snatched all their souls. The stirring perils of the previous day, the reckless way in which their wild craft went plunging towards its flying mark; by all these things, their hearts were struck together. They were one man, not thirty. For as the one ship that held them all, all the individualities of the crew, this man's valor, that man's fear, all varieties were welded into oneness, and were all directed to that fatal goal which Ahab their lord pointed to.

How they still strove through that infinite blueness to seek out the thing that might destroy them!

"Sing out for him, if ye see him!" cried Ahab.

"There she breaches! There she breaches!" was the cry. "Aye, breach your last to the sun, Moby Dick!" cried Ahab, "thy hour is at hand[157]".

---

157 Behold, the hour is at hand, and the Son of Man is betrayed in the hands of sinners. Matthew 26:45.

Unmindful of the tedious rope ladders, the men, like shooting stars, slid to the deck; while Ahab, less dartingly, but still rapidly was dropped from his perch.

"Lower away," he cried, and soon reached his boat, a spare one rigged the prior afternoon.

As if to strike a quick terror into them, Moby Dick had turned, and was now coming for the three crews. Ahab's boat was central; and cheering his men, he told them he would take the whale head to head. But the White Whale churning himself into furious speed, rushed the boats with open jaws and a lashing tail, battling on every side, unaffected by the irons darting at him from every boat.

The White Whale so crossed and recrossed and in a thousand ways entangled the slack of the three lines now connected to him. Caught and twisted, corkscrewed in the mazes of the line, loose harpoons and lances came flashing and dripping up to the bows of Ahab's boat. Only one thing could be done. Seizing the boat knife, he cut the rope near the deck, dropping the cluster of steel into the sea. That instant, the White Whale made a sudden rush among the remaining tangles of the other lines, dragging the boats of Stubb and Flask towards his tail, dashing them together like two rolling coconuts on a surf beaten beach, and then, diving down in to the sea, disappeared in a boiling whirlpool.

While the two crews were yet circling in the waters, reaching out after the oars and other floating furniture, little Flask bobbed up and down like an empty vial, twitching his legs upwards to escape the dreaded jaws of sharks; and Stubb was singing out for someone to ladle him up. Ahab's yet unstricken boat seemed drawn up towards Heaven by invisible wires, when the White Whale dashed his broad forehead against its bottom and sent it, turning over and over into the air, till it fell again, and Ahab and his men struggled out from under it.

As before, the attentive Pequod, having witnessed the whole fight, again came bearing down to the rescue, picked up the floating mariners, tubs, oars and whatever else could be snatched, and safely landed them on her decks. Some sprained shoulders, wrists, and ankles, contusions; wrenched harpoons and lances, inextricable bundles of rope; shattered oars and plans; all these were there; but no fatal or even serious ill seemed to have befallen anyone.

Ahab was now found grimly clinging to his boat's broken half, which afforded a comparatively easy float; it didn't exhaust him as the previous day's mishap. But when he was helped to the deck, all eyes were fastened upon him; as he half hung upon the shoulder of Starbuck, who had thus far been the foremost to assist him. His ivory leg had been snapped off, leaving but one short sharp splinter.

"But no bones broken, sir, I hope" said Stubb with true concern.

"Aye! And all splintered to pieces, Stubb! But even with a broken bone, old Ahab is untouched; and I account no living bone of mine more important than the dead one that is lost."

"Mr. Starbuck down the rest of the spare boats and rig them, and muster the boat's crews."

"Great God! But for one single instant slow yourself," cried Starbuck; "never, never wilt thou capture him, old man, in Jesus' name no more of this, that's worse than the devil's madness. Two days chased; twice broken to splinters; your very leg once more snatched from under thee; all good angels warning you to stop."

"What more do you want? Should we keep chasing this murderous fish till he swamps the last man? Should we be dragged by him to the bottom of the sea? Should we be towed by him to the infernal world? Oh, oh, Impiety and blasphemy to hunt him more!"

"Starbuck, of late I've felt strangely moved to you; trusting you. But in this matter of the whale, Ahab is for ever Ahab, man. You see an old man cut down to the stump; leaning on a shivered lance; propped up on a lonely foot. 'Tis Ahab, his body's part; but Ahab's soul's a centipede that moves upon a hundred legs. I feel strained, half stranded. Moby Dick, two days he's floated, tomorrow will be the third. Aye, men, he'll rise once more, but only to spout his last! Do you feel brave men, brave?"

"As fearless fire," cried Stubb.

"And as mechanical," muttered Ahab.

When dusk descended, the whale was still in sight.

So once more the sail was shortened, and everything passed nearly as on the previous night. Meantime, of the broken wood of Ahab's wrecked craft the carpenter made him another leg; while slouched Ahab stood fixed within his cabin.

Chapter 40. The Chase - The Third Day

The morning of the third day dawned fair and fresh.

"Do you see him?" cried Ahab; but the whale was not yet in sight.

"Follow that wake, that's all, steady as thou goest. What a lovely day again! A fairer day could not dawn upon the world. Here's food for thought, had Ahab time to think; but Ahab never thinks; he only feels, feels, feels. Were I the wind, I'd blow no more on such a wicked, miserable world. I'd crawl somewhere to a cave, and slink there. Yet, 'tis a noble and heroic thing, the wind! Who ever conquered it?"

"Aloft there, what do you see?"

"Nothing sir."

"Nothing! And noon is at hand! See the sun! Aye, aye, it must be so. I've oversailed him. Aye, he's chasing ME now; not I, HIM. That's bad; I might have known it, too."

"Against the wind he now steers for the open jaw," murmured Starbuck to himself, as he coiled against the rail. "God keep us, but already my bones feel damp within me, and from the inside wet my flesh. I disobey my God by obeying him!"

"Sway me up!" cried Ahab, advancing to the fiber basket. "We should meet him soon." "Aye, aye, sir," and straightway Starbuck did Ahab's bidding, and once more Ahab swung on high.

A whole hour now passed. Time itself now held long breaths with keen suspense. But at last, off of the bow, Ahab spotted the spout again.

"Forehead to forehead I meet thee, this third time, Moby Dick! He travels fast and I must get down. But let me have one more good round look up here at the sea; there's time for that. An old, old sight, and yet somehow so young; aye, and not changed a wink since I first saw it, a boy from the sand-hills of Nantucket! The same to Noah and to me. Goodbye, goodbye old boat! For you and I, old boat, we both grow old together, minus a leg that's all. By heaven this dead wood is better than my live flesh, in every way. I've known some ships made of dead trees that outlast the lives of men made of the most vital stuff. Goodbye Pequod, keep a good eye upon the whale when I'm gone."

He gave the word and was steadily lowered through the blue air to the deck.

In due time the boats were lowered; but standing on the stern, Ahab hovered to the point of descent and waved to his mate, who held one of the tackle ropes on deck.

"Starbuck!"

"Sir?"

"For the third time my soul's ship starts upon this voyage, Starbuck."

"Yes sir, thou wilt have it so."

"Starbuck. I am old; shake hands with me, man." Their hands met; their eyes fastened; Starbuck's tears, the glue.

"Oh, my captain, my captain! Go not! Go not! See, it's a brave man that weeps[158]."

"Lower away!" cried Ahab, tossing the mate's arm from him. "Stand by the crew." In an instant the boat was pulling around.

"The sharks! The sharks! Cried a voice from the low cabin window; "O master, my master, come back!"

But Ahab heard nothing; and the boat leaped on.

Yet the voice spake true; for scarce had he pushed from the ship, when numbers of sharks, rising from out of the dark waters beneath the hull, maliciously snapped at the blades of the oars, every time they dipped in the water; and in this way accompanied the boat with their bites.

---

158 John 11:35: "Jesus Wept."

"Heart of steel!" murmured Starbuck gazing over the side, and following with his eyes the receding boat. "Oh! My God! What is this that shoots through me, and leaves me so deadly calm, yet expectant. Future things swim before me, all the past is somehow grown dim. All the problems of life are clearing, but clouds sweep between, is my journey's end coming?"

Suddenly the waters around them slowly swelled in broad circles; then quickly upheaved, rising to the surface. A low rumbling sound was heard; and then all held their breaths. Shrouded in a thin veil of mist, a vast form shot from the sea, it hovered for a moment in the air and then fell back into the deep.

"Give way!" cried Ahab to the oarsmen, and the boats darted forward to the attack; but maddened by yesterday's fresh irons that corroded in him, Moby Dick seemed possessed by all the angels that fell from heaven. He came churning his tail among the boats; and once more flailed them apart; sending the irons and lances from the boats, but leaving Ahab's almost without a scar.

"Away mates, to the ship! Those boats are useless now. Down, men! The first thing that but offers to jump from this boat I stand in, that thing I harpoon. Ye are not other men, but my arms and my legs; and so obey me. Where's the whale? Gone down again?"

Moby Dick was now again steadily swimming forward; and had almost passed the ship. He seemed swimming with his utmost velocity, and now only intent upon pursuing his own straight path in the sea.

"Oh Ahab," cried Starbuck, "not too late is it, even now the third day, to desist. See! Moby Dick seeks thee not. It is thou, thou, that madly seekest him!"

Yet, as Ahab glided over the waves the merciless sharks accompanied him; and so continually bit at the oars, that the blades became jagged and crunched, and left small splinters in the sea, at almost every dip.

"Heed them not! Pull on!"

"But sir, the thin blades grow smaller and smaller!"

"They will last long enough! Pull on!" He muttered. "Who can tell whether these sharks swim to feast on the whale or on Ahab? But pull on! We are near him."

At length the craft was cast to one side, and ran along the whale's flank, Ahab was fairly close to him; when, with body arched back and both arms high lifted to the poise, he darted his fierce iron, and his far fiercer curse into the hated whale. As both steel and curse sank in the flesh, Moby Dick sideways writhed, spasmodically rolled against the bow and so suddenly turned the boat over that had it not been for the elevated part that he clung to, Ahab would once more have been tossed into the sea.

As it was, three of the oarsmen were flung out; but two of them with a rising wave hurled themselves onboard again; the third man helplessly still afloat and swimming.

Almost simultaneously, with a mighty volition, the White Whale darted through the turbulent sea. But when Ahab cried out to the steersman to hold the line, and commanded the crew to turn around on their seats and tow the boat up to the whale, at that moment the treacherous line felt the strain and snapped in the empty air.

"What breaks in me? Some sinew cracks! Oars! Oars! Burst in upon him!"

"Oars! Oars! Slope downwards to thy depths, O sea, that ere it be for ever too late, Ahab may slide this last time upon the Whale! I see the ship! Dash on, my men! Will ye not save my ship?"

But as the oarsmen violently forced their boat through the sledge hammering seas, the disabled boat lay nearly level with the waves; its half-wading, splashing crew, trying hard to stop the gap and bale out the pouring water.

Starbuck and Stubb, standing on the bow beneath, caught sight of the coming monster.

"The whale, the whale! Oh, all ye sweet powers of air, now hug me close! Let not Starbuck die. Oar on, I say, ye fools, the jaw! The jaw! Is this the end of all my bursting prayers? My God, stand by me now!"

"Stand not by me, but stand under me, whoever you are that will now help. I grin at thee, thou grinning whale!"

From the ship's bows, nearly all the seamen now hung inactive; hammers, lances, and harpoons mechanically retained in their hands; all their enchanted eyes intent upon the whale. Retribution, swift vengeance, eternal malice were in his soul, and despite all mortal man could do, the solid white forehead smote the ship's starboard bow, till men and timbers reeled.

Driving beneath the ship, the whale ran along its keel; but turning under water, swiftly shot to the surface again, within a few yards of Ahab's boat.

"Towards thee, I roll, thou all-destroying but unconquering whale; to the last, I grapple with thee; from hell's heart I stab at thee; for hate's sake I spit my last breath at thee. Let me then break to pieces while chasing thee, though tied to thee, thou damned whale! THUS, I give up the spear!"

Ahab darted his harpoon which struck the fleeing whale, and with igniting velocity the line caught, tangled and then wrapped around Ahab's neck and he was voicelessly shot out of the boat. The crew didn't even know he was gone. The rope's final end flew out of the empty boat, knocked down an oarsman, and smiting the sea, disappeared in its depths.

For an instant, the boat's crew stood tranced, then turned. "The ship? Great God, where is the ship?" Soon they saw her along the fading horizon, as in the gaseous Fata Morgana[159]; only the upper masts out of the water, the pagan harpooners still maintained their lookouts on the sea.

And now, whirlpool circles seized the boat and all its crew, and each floating oar, and every lance pole, and spinning all around and round in one vortex, carried the last of the Pequod out of sight, except for the few inches of mast and flag that remained visible above the water. A sky-hawk had tauntingly followed the ship from its natural home among the stars and was pecking at the flag when its broad fluttering wing caught the mast and was held in a death grasp and submerged; and so the bird of heaven's form folded in the flag of Ahab, and went down with his ship, which like Satan, would not sink to hell till she had dragged a living part of heaven along with her.

Now small fowls flew screaming over the yawning gulf; a sullen white surf beat against its steep sides, then all collapsed, and the great shroud of the sea rolled on as it rolled five thousand years ago.

---

159 A term for when atmospheric conditions at sea cause optical illusions in the horizon, making shapes seem taller and more distorted.

Epilogue

I ONLY ESCAPED TO TELL THEE

The drama's done. Why then does anyone step forth? Because one did survive the wreck.

It so happened that I was he whom the Fates ordained to take the place of Ahab's bowsman and who, on the last day the three men were tossed from out of the rocking boat, was dropped astern. So floating on the margins of the ensuing scene, and in full sight of it, I was slowly drawn towards the suctioning and closing vortex. Round and round I did revolve till gaining the vital center and now liberated by reason of its cunning spring and owing to its great buoyancy the coffin life-buoy shot lengthwise from the sea, fell over and floated by my side.

Buoyed up by that coffin, for almost one whole day and night, I floated on a soft and hallowed current. The unharming sharks glided by as if with padlocks on their mouths; the savage sea-hawks sailed with sheathed beaks. On the second day, a sail drew near, nearer, and picked me up at last. It was the devious cruising Rachel[160], that in her retracing search after her missing children, only found another orphan.

---

160 Thus saith the Lord; refrain thy voice from weeping, and thine eyes from tears; for thy work shall be rewarded, and there is hope in thine end that thy children shall return." Jeremiah 31:16-17.

The End

"And the great shroud of the sea rolled on as it rolled five thousand years ago".

*Please see Levi F. Barber's other illustrated Moby Dick book

"He Called Me Ishmael" which you can find here on Amazon.

Find More Decent Books at:

Citations

Footnote 5: "Perhaps the most uncomfortable infliction that the two orchard thieves entailed upon us." (2013, October 26). Chasing Flukes. https://chasingflukes.com/reading_guide-overview/glossary-contents/1orchard-thieves/

Footnote 6: Erik, V. A. P. B. (2015, August 29). Be Smart, Don't Fart: The Pythagorean Prohibition of Beans. SENTENTIAE ANTIQUAE. https://sententiaeantiquae.com/2015/08/31/be-smart-dont-fart-the-pythagorean-prohibition-of-beans/

Footnote 7: Roseblatt, R. (1980, January 28). Call Us Ishmael. Washington Post. https://www.washingtonpost.com/archive/politics/1980/01/28/call-us-ishmael/c98b27f0-c1af-437e-8d1e-8268116445c7/

Footnote 22: Friedrich, G. (1965). Project MUSE - A Note on Quakerism and Moby Dick: Hawthorne's "The Gentle Boy" as a Possible Source. Friedrich. https://muse.jhu.edu/article/394363/summary

Footnote 47: Annotations and Commentary on Moby Dick. (2020). Evelyn C. Leeper. http://leepers.us/evelyn/moby1.htm

Footnote 63: Updike, J. (2019, July 31). Herman Melville's Soft Withdrawal. The New Yorker. https://www.newyorker.com/magazine/1982/05/10/melvilles-withdrawal

Footnote 72: Hoare, P. (2019, July 30). Subversive, queer and terrifyingly relevant: six reasons why Moby-Dick is the novel for our times. The Guardian. https://www.theguardian.com/books/2019/jul/30/subversive-queer-and-terrifyingly-relevant-six-reasons-why-moby-dick-is-the-novel-for-our-times

Footnote 73: King, G. (2013, March 1). The True-Life Horror That Inspired Moby-Dick. Smithsonian Magazine. https://www.smithsonianmag.com/history/the-true-life-horror-that-inspired-moby-dick-17576/

Footnote 75: Benzel, J. (2017, July 12). Sag Harbor, N.Y.: Celebrities and Small-Town Aura. The New York Times. https://www.nytimes.com/2017/07/12/realestate/sag-harbor-ny-celebrities-and-small-town-aura.html

Footnote 85: Macy, O., & Macy, W. C. (2018). The History Of Nantucket: Being A Compendious Account Of The First Settlement Of The Island By The English, Together With The Rise And Progress Of The Whale Fishery. Franklin Classics.

Footnote 117: Moby Dick, Myth, and Classical Moralism: Bulkington as HerculesJonathan Cook, Leviathan5.1 (2003):

Footnote 148: The All of the If. (1997, March 17). The New Republic. https://newrepublic.com/article/122388/all-if-james-wood-life-herman-melville

Footnote 153: Milton, J., & Leonard, J. (2003). Paradise Lost (Penguin Classics) (1st ed.). Penguin Classics.

Made in United States
North Haven, CT
18 June 2023

37921442R00061